LOOK OUT FOR THE
FITZGERALD-
TROUTS

# LOOK OUT FOR THE FITZGERALD-TROUTS

## ESTA SPALDING

illustrated by

## SYDNEY SMITH

LITTLE, BROWN AND COMPANY

New York Boston

Copyright © 2016 by Esta Spalding
Illustrations copyright © 2016 by Sydney Smith
Excerpt from *Knock About with the Fitzgerald-Trouts* copyright
© 2017 by Esta Spalding

Cover design by Sasha Illingworth
Cover illustration copyright © 2016 by Sydney Smith. Lettering by Grey318.
Cover copyright © 2016 by Hachette Book Group, Inc.

Little, Brown and Company
Hachette Book Group
1290 Avenue of the Americas, New York, NY 10104
Visit us at lb-kids.com

Originally published in hardcover and ebook by Little, Brown and Company
in May 2016 | First Trade Paperback Edition: April 2017

Little, Brown and Company is a division of Hachette Book Group, Inc.
The Little, Brown name and logo are trademarks of Hachette Book Group, Inc.

The publisher is not responsible for websites (or their content)
that are not owned by the publisher

The Library of Congress has cataloged the hardcover edition as follows:
Names: Spalding, Esta, author.
Title: Look out for the Fitzgerald-Trouts / by Esta Spalding.
Description: First edition. | New York ; Boston : Little, Brown and Company, 2016.
| Summary: "The Fitzgerald-Trouts are four barely related siblings living together
in a small car on a lush tropical island, but when they begin to outgrow their small
vehicle, they must band together to find a new home"—Provided by publisher.
Identifiers: LCCN 2015020621| ISBN 9780316298582 (hardback) |
ISBN 9780316298599 (ebook) | ISBN 9780316298568 (library edition ebook)
Subjects: | CYAC: Homeless persons—Fiction. | Brothers and sisters—Fiction. |
Families—Fiction. | Automobiles—Fiction. | Islands—Fiction. | BISAC:
JUVENILE FICTION / Family / Siblings. | JUVENILE FICTION / Social Issues
/ Adolescence. | JUVENILE FICTION / Social Issues / Emotions & Feelings.
Classification: LCC PZ7.1.S713 Lo 2016 | DDC [Fic]—dc23
LC record available at http://lccn.loc.gov/2015020621

ISBNs: 978-0-316-29857-5 (paperback); 978-0-316-29859-9 (ebook)

Printed in the United States of America

LSC-C

10 9 8 7 6 5 4 3 2 1

*For Gemma, who gave notes*

# CHAPTER
## 1

For many years the four Fitzgerald-Trout children—Kim, Kimo, Pippa, and Toby— lived happily in the little green car in the parking lot beside the beach. But all that came to an end one Saturday when the sun rose over the ocean and its light shone through the windshield of the car where the Fitzgerald-Trout children had slept very badly. Badly enough to change everything.

Kim, who was eleven and the oldest of the children, had tossed and turned trying to stretch out in her seat behind the steering wheel. She had spent most of her sleepless night thinking about how she wanted to live in a real house with a real bed.

Kimo, much wider than Kim, with a broad back and shoulders, had had an even worse night's sleep, but because he was more practical, he hadn't spent the night dreaming of a bed; he spent the night fiddling with the knob of his seat, trying to get it to tilt farther back. It hadn't worked, and now he climbed out of the car, stretching in the morning light and rubbing his cramped arms and legs. Kim joined him and they left Pippa and Toby, the youngest two Fitzgerald-Trouts, tossing and turning in the backseat, where they too had spent a long, sleepless night.

As Kim quietly opened the trunk of the car to retrieve her toothbrush and toothpaste, she found that she was thinking—for maybe the millionth time—about the Perfects. They were a family of four wonderful children in Kim's favorite book. The Perfects lived in a stately house on a suburban street where mothers pushed strollers and fathers taught kite-flying in the park. *The Perfects* was so precious to Kim that she kept the book close to her at all times, either in the glove compartment of the car or under the front seat. Kim wished that her family could be just like the Perfects, but then she looked at Kimo, with his finger in his ear cleaning out the wax, and at the car, where the youngest two were crammed in the backseat sleeping. She knew her family was nothing like the Perfects.

She also knew things could have been much worse. After all, their little green car wasn't parked in a dark alley or beside a strip mall; it was parked at one of the many long, sandy beaches on the tropical island that the Fitzgerald-Trouts called home. The island wasn't very big. There was a road around its edge and anyone could drive that road and circle the whole island in about four hours. The road ran right beside the coast except for one place where it veered inland to avoid a forest: the Sakahatchi Forest. Island legend had it that deep in the Sakahatchi, bloodsucking iguanas roosted in the trees, but no one knew if this was really true or not. Islanders avoided the Sakahatchi and spent their time in the many towns that were filled with shops, restaurants, and shaved ice stands, or they went to one of the island's many beaches or hiked on one of its volcanic mountains. Except for the Sakahatchi Forest, it really was a very pleasant island, and people from all over the world flew long distances across the ocean to visit it.

But Kim had never lived anywhere else so it was easy to forget how idyllic the island and the beach were and spend her time worrying instead. Every day when Kim woke up she pulled out of her pocket the little notebook that held her list of all the things that needed to be done. Her list that day was pretty long. It looked like this:

*Brush teeth*
*Brush hair*

*Make breakfast*
*Get groceries*
*Ice for cooler*
*Gas*
*Sandwiches for lunch*
*Fix Pippa's glasses*
*Campfire dinner*
*Find a house*

On a day when she hadn't slept well because the little car they lived in was cramped and crowded, that last item on her list—find a house—felt particularly urgent to Kim.

Kim also kept a list of things for Kimo to do and she was always reminding him of what he had not yet done. That morning, standing beside the trunk of the car, Kim showed Kimo his list. It looked like this:

*Replace trunk lightbulb*
*Do dishes*

*Scrub cooler*
*Collect kindling*
*Teach Toby to write his name*
*Catch a fish*

Kimo's list always included having to catch a fish. Luckily for him, the ocean had every kind of sea creature living in it and was an endless source of food. Of course, when fish got too boring to eat, the children would get in the car and drive to the foot of Mount Muldoon, where fruits of every flavor could be found if they were willing to walk, which wasn't so easy since none of the children on that island, even the ones who lived in houses, ever wore shoes. The mud would squinch between the children's toes as they climbed the steep uphill trail. It would get so muddy that sometimes they had to grab on to branches to stop from sliding, and sometimes even Kimo, who was very sure-footed, fell facedown in the muck. But it was worth it, because the fruits, which grew from trees and bushes at the top of the mountain, tasted more delicious than anything they could buy at any of the sweetshops on the island.

Even if the children weren't hungry, the walk was worth it because on the way they would see wonderful things. There were waterfalls on the mountain and trees with leaves the size of garbage can lids. There were exotic flowers that attracted birds so small they could fit in a match-box. I know this because Pippa Fitzgerald-Trout kept just such a matchbox in her pocket and in it the tiny body of just such a bird. She'd once taken it to school for show-and-tell, and it says some-thing about that island that none of the children she showed it to were surprised by it at all. In fact, several of them had matchboxes and birds in their pockets too.

While Kim went to the beach's public bathroom to brush her teeth and worry about things, Kimo, who always slept with his swim trunks on, was walking down toward the edge of the ocean. When he got there, he didn't hesitate, but splashed right in and dove through a wave, sinking to the ocean floor. He lay there staring up through the blue water at the sky.

It was at times like these, when he had escaped from the cramped car and was alone in the ocean holding his breath, that Kimo let himself think about his father. Kimo's father, Johnny Trout, had been missing at sea since Kimo was little.

What Kimo had learned about his father from one of his teachers at school was that Johnny Trout was descended from the island's first settlers, from the first tribe to ever fish in that ocean or set foot in those mountains—hundreds and hundreds of years ago. The teacher said there was still a lot of argument among island historians about how those first people got to that island. Did they come from *this* country across the ocean in the east or *that* country across the ocean in the west? And whichever country they came from, how did they travel such a long distance across such a large ocean in their wooden sailing canoes? Some historians thought there was another explanation entirely.

The historians met at the Royal Palm, which was the island's fanciest hotel, to argue their opinions. But Johnny Trout had thought the arguments were ridiculous. How could such a problem be solved at a fancy hotel? Instead, he had flown to the distant country in the west, where he found a large tree, carved out his own boat, and set sail, heading back toward the island. Before he left, he told people that he hoped once and for all to prove how his people had originally come to the island.

But that was the last time he was ever seen, so perhaps Johnny Trout had been wrong.

Stretched out on the bottom of the ocean, looking up at the sky, Kimo thought about his father and hoped he was a castaway on some island and was swimming in that same ocean right now. With the last bit of air burning in his lungs, Kimo wondered if someday he and his father would meet.

He pushed off the sandy bottom and shot straight up, popping into the air and taking a deep breath. A few minutes later he walked, dripping wet, up the beach and joined Kim back at the car to make breakfast.

They did the same thing every morning. First they opened the trunk of the car and pulled out a box of cereal and the cooler that was filled with ice. Then Kim set four bowls on top of the car's roof and Kimo filled the bowls with the cereal. He got the milk out of the cooler (he noticed today that the ice was almost all melted) and poured the milk into each of the four bowls. They both liked it when they worked like this—communicating almost telepathically.

Kim had always thought of the two of them as kind of like twins. After all, weren't they born only a few months apart? And though they'd been born to completely different sets of parents, in completely different hospitals, on different sides of that island, she had been named Kim and he had been named Kimo. Only one letter different. It was as if, even then, before they were brother and sister, some invisible thread had joined them.

When the cereal was ready and there was a spoon in each bowl, Kim tapped on the car's back windows to tell Pippa and Toby it was time to eat.

Toby and Pippa climbed out of the car,

stretching their sore arms and legs. Pippa, who was eight, with brown freckles that made her face look polka-dotted, reached into a compartment in one of the car's doors and took out her glasses. She had found them in the glove compartment several months before. They were cracked in places and a little bit bent, but she had decided that she should wear them because they made the edges of leaves on the trees look sharper. Now when she put them on, her head felt sore, and she rubbed her hand over it and found a lump as big as a mushimush berry. "My head has a bump," she said, scowling. "Like someone hit it with a coconut."

"Who would hit it with a coconut?" Kim asked, wary of upsetting Pippa, who had a terrible temper and whose freckles made her look like she was about to explode.

"I don't know!" Pippa growled.

"I have a bump too," said Toby. He was five years old, with dark hair like Kimo's and bright green eyes like Pippa's. He rarely said a word, so when he did, the others took it seriously.

"What happened?" asked Kim, taking him seriously.

"Dunno," said Toby, "but it hurts."

The cereal in their bowls was getting soggy as they stood there rubbing their heads. Watching them, a terrible question nudged its way into Kim's own head. It was a question that she didn't dare ask out loud. What if Pippa's and Toby's heads hurt because they had been bumping against each other all night? What if the two littlest Fitzgerald-Trouts had outgrown the backseat of the car? If that was true, everything would have to change for them. But who would change it? And how? Now Kim had these new unanswered questions to worry about too.

All day long Kim felt these questions running in circles around her brain. She felt them circling while the Fitzgerald-Trouts washed the breakfast dishes in the ocean, scrubbing them with sand instead of soap. She felt them circling while they swam. She felt them circling while they went to the gas station to buy more ice for the cooler and to fill up the gas tank. She felt them while they swung on the tire swing at the playground near the beach. She felt them while she fixed Pippa's glasses with a little bit of duct tape. She even felt them while she sat on a picnic bench at the beach eating shaved ice covered in coconut syrup. Kimo must have noticed her mood because when he was done with his shaved ice, he scooped Kim up in the air so that her arms and legs were wiggling like an insect's, and he danced around the picnic table with her, shouting in his best phony British accent, "Things are looking up." Though this amused Toby and Pippa (who loved Kimo's strongman antics), Kim barely cracked a smile. By the time they were grilling fish over their campfire, Kim was so tired of trying to ignore the circling questions that she decided she needed to fill her brain with something else. "Let's go to the drive-in," she said.

So they drove the little green car to the drive-in and watched an old movie about giant ants taking over planet Earth. The movie terrified all of them except Pippa, who laughed whenever a grown-up was eaten by one of the ants. (The only thing more terrifying than Pippa's temper was her sense of humor.) Watching the movie, Kim thought, life could be worse; at least our island isn't being invaded by giant ants. But when they got back to the beach and climbed into their places to sleep, the circling questions came back and there was no getting rid of them.

"Ouch," said Pippa as Toby lay down on the backseat beside her. "Move your head."

"Move it where?" asked Toby.

"I don't know," said Pippa, "but it doesn't fit."

"He can't just take off his head," Kimo offered from the front seat.

"We're too crammed in back here," Pippa complained, and then she added the words that Kim had been dreading: "We don't fit anymore."

Before Kim could contradict her, Toby burst into tears and said, "What happens if I don't fit?"

Kim turned around in her seat and mopped up his tears with a tissue. She had no idea how to answer him. She couldn't offer to sleep in the back...that would make things worse. And there wasn't room for Toby with her in the front. If they took all their clothes and suitcases and food and books and the cooler out of the trunk, could one of them sleep there?

She heard Kimo's door swing open, and she turned to look. He was climbing out of the car. "Take my seat," he said to Toby.

"Really?" gurgled Toby, snot coming out of his nose. "What will you do?"

"I'll figure something out." As Toby crawled up into the front, Kimo looked over toward the forest and then down toward the moonlit beach. The sand makes a better bed than the leaves, he thought, and so he headed that way.

"You can have my seat if you want," Kim called out her window to him, half hoping he wouldn't take her up on the offer.

"I'm okay," said Kimo.

When he got to the sand, he lay down and wiggled around until he'd made a comfortable nest. Then he turned to look at the stars. He was wondering if his father was sleeping on a beach somewhere too. He hoped he was. It's not bad, he thought, and then, with a sigh, I hope it doesn't rain.

Tilted back in her seat in the car, Kim pulled out her copy of *The Perfects*. It was an old book with thick, rough pages. Rubbing her index finger over it in the dark, Kim could feel the outline of the tall house that was imprinted on the cloth cover. Inside that house were the bedrooms with the beds where the four Perfect children slept, dreaming their perfect dreams. But there was something very unusual about that book: If you flipped the book over and turned it around, what had once been the back cover of the book became the front cover, and that cover said *The Awfuls* and had a rough little shack imprinted on it. In other words, depending on which side you started from, the book told two completely different stories—one about the Perfect family and one about the Awful family. Kim never, ever reread the Awfuls' side of the book. She wished that side didn't exist, and she thought the author of the book—Stella Spalding—had made a terrible mistake in writing it. Many times Kim had considered tearing the Awfuls' half of the book from the spine and tossing it in the garbage, but she loved books too much to destroy even one that made her so queasy. Instead, she kept the Perfects' side faceup and focused on reading and rereading that tale.

Now, sitting in the car, cloaked in darkness,

Kim ran her fingers over the Perfects' house and promised herself that she would move the bottom item on her to-do list up to the top. I must find us a house, she thought as she tumbled into sleep.

CHAPTER
2

Before we get to the shocking events of the rainy Sunday after the night Kimo slept on the beach, I should explain to you very simply how the Fitzgerald-Trout children were related. Unfortunately nothing about the Fitzgerald-Trouts was simple. For one thing, the children didn't all have the same father. Kim, Pippa, and Toby shared a father and were all Fitzgeralds, but Kimo had a different father and was the only Trout. Long ago someone had decided that all the children should be called Fitzgerald-Trout and so that is what was written on their report cards and that is what they called themselves.

As for the children's mothers, the girls shared one and the boys shared another. From time to time one of the mothers would find the car wherever it was parked and would stop by to make them wash their hands and to tell them to do their homework and, sometimes, to give them some money. Then she would be off again, saying, "I must be going, I'm terribly busy," and the children would breathe a sigh of relief. They knew the mothers weren't terribly busy, they were just busy being terrible. But who cared? The children liked their independence and having a terrible mother (or two terrible mothers) who were around all the time would not have suited them at all.

The girls' mother was named Maya and it would be hard to imagine someone greedier than she was. She was so greedy that she wore diamonds all over herself, even on her clothes. She wore so many diamonds that in the sunlight she was impossible to look at. Pippa took off her glasses whenever Maya visited because she said her mother made her eyes hurt. But that wasn't the worst thing about Maya. The worst thing was that even though she was rich, she only ever gave the children her loose change. How were they supposed to buy food and clothes and gas for the car with only loose change?

The boys' mother, Tina, was not nearly so greedy. In fact, she dropped off money promptly every month and it was always enough for the children to buy groceries and schoolbooks and sometimes even new clothes. She might not have been cheap, but Tina was terribly vain. She wore tight little skirts and yellow snakeskin cowboy boots, and she had a bouffant hairdo that stood six whole inches above her head.

At least once during every single visit to the car, Tina checked her reflection in the side-view mirror. Kimo had made a game out of guessing how many times during a visit Tina would do this. There had been one visit when she looked at herself seventeen times!

As if Tina's vanity weren't bad enough, she always made the children feel bad about how *they* looked. She would tell Kim that she needed to brush her hair, and Kimo that he needed to bathe, and Pippa to sit up straight, and Toby that he must wipe his nose. A visit from Tina made the children want to cover the mirrors in their car and never check their own reflections again. It was always a relief when she smeared on her lipstick, checked her reflection one last time, and said, "I've got to go, I'm terribly busy." As soon as she was gone, Pippa would quip, "Lucky for us her schedule is chockablock." They would not have wanted Tina to be any less busy.

With four parents to choose from, you'd think there would be one who was worthy of raising the Fitzgerald-Trout children. But I can testify that none of them were. Certainly not the terrible mothers. Not Kimo's father (Mr. Trout), who was missing at sea. And not even Dr. Fitzgerald, though he had at one time at least tried to take care of all four of them.

Dr. Fitzgerald was a scientist who studied rare mammals, and the older children remembered him living in the little green car with them. In fact, if Kim remembered right, living in the car had been Dr. Fitzgerald's idea. Kim told the story like this. One day, when Kim was in first grade, Dr. Fitzgerald had picked her and Kimo up from school and told them they were going for a ride. When they got to the car it was loaded with the youngest two Fitzgerald-Trouts (which was normal) but also with bags, boxes, and suitcases (which was not).

"What's that stuff?" Kim asked.

"That's my equipment," Dr. Fitzgerald answered with a grin. "I'm going to track the island's rare mammals while I keep track of you four!"

Kim didn't remember ever sleeping anywhere but the car again, and she had no idea what had become of the house they once called home. Neither she nor Kimo even remembered where it was.

Life with Dr. Fitzgerald wasn't any fun. "We were tucked in at night on top of microscopes, tripods, and cameras," Kim reminded Pippa and Toby. "It was very uncomfortable." If nighttime in the car was bad, daytime was even worse. During the day, Dr. Fitzgerald kept them out of school so that they could help him do his research.

"You'll learn more from this than you will in any classroom," he cackled, but neither Kim nor Kimo remembered learning a thing. What they remembered was that he became obsessed with the island's population of rare pygmy possums and took the children on long hikes to track and identify them. During these outings, Kim and Kimo carried not only Pippa and Toby in their arms but also heavy packs on their backs filled with Dr. Fitzgerald's equipment.

"Look out! Be careful!" he'd shout at them as they struggled up a particularly steep hillside.

"He wasn't shouting because he thought we might hurt ourselves," Kim told the youngest two. "He was shouting because he thought we might hurt *his equipment*."

Kim didn't remember her father ever spotting a single pygmy possum during all those miles of hiking. What she did remember was how happy she had felt when a large group of pygmy possums had been sighted on a different, distant island, and Dr. Fitzgerald had packed up his gear and flown there. After that, the Fitzgerald-Trouts were the envy of all their school friends because without parents they had a great deal of freedom. They also had Dr. Fitzgerald's car.

Just before he left the island, Dr. Fitzgerald

decided to teach one of the children to drive. He knew they would need a way to get around in the car once he was gone. Though Kim was rather young, she was the eldest and the most natural choice for driver because she could be counted on to take charge. Dr. Fitzgerald sat Kim down in the front seat and told her to turn the key. She did so with ease, but when he told her to put her foot on the brake, her foot just dangled in the air. It was Pippa who pointed and shouted, "Her feet don't even reach the pedals!"

"Let me try," said Kimo, who was only a few months younger. Hoping Kim would let him take her place, he didn't push her or poke her, and Kim climbed out of the car, giving him a turn in the front seat. Much to Kim's relief, Kimo's legs were shorter than hers. If anyone was going to drive, it would have to be Kim.

But how would she drive the car if she couldn't reach the pedals?

They all stood there a moment, looking from Kim's legs to the car and back again. What would they do? Suddenly Dr. Fitzgerald exclaimed, "Eureka!"

He began to unlace his high-top sneakers (because he was a grown-up, he owned several pairs of shoes) and when he was done he offered them to Kim, who stared at them, having no idea how they would help her drive. But when her father reached into the car's trunk and got out the duct tape and two cans of beef stew, she understood perfectly.

Those stew cans taped to the shoes lengthened her legs just enough that she could reach the pedals.

Kim took to driving with ease—as most children would if their parents would ever let them try. She was careful to steer properly and always braked at stop signs and traffic lights and for crossing puk-puk geese, which was the law on that island. She was mindful not to drive too fast or too close to other cars, she always remembered to put her turn signal on thirty feet before she planned to turn, and she knew not to park beneath a mushi-mush tree. She always sat on a pile of books so that she could see over the dashboard, but even though Kim loved reading more than anything, she never read while she was driving. In all ways she really was a very lawful and competent driver.

After Dr. Fitzgerald left, the children settled into life as a happy family of four. Of course, as happens in some families, not all of them were actually related.

Kim and Pippa didn't share any DNA with Kimo at all. They had different mothers and different fathers. But they knew that didn't matter. They were a family because if you aren't a family, you don't live together in the same little car. They knew they were brothers and sisters, even if when they made a new friend at school they had to take out a stick and draw in the dirt to explain just how they were related.

CHAPTER
3

I'm sick to death of Sorry!" Pippa was shouting, but none of the others could hear her because they were all shouting too—even Toby. It was a terrible day: the day after the night Kimo slept on the beach. The rainy Sunday. Because it was raining, the children were stuck in the car, playing game after game of Sorry! It was a game they usually liked because, like most of us, they hated to say "Sorry" when they were supposed to, but loved to say it when they didn't mean it. "Sorry!" they would say as they knocked one another's pieces back to the start. "Sorry!" as they skipped ahead of the others, and then, "Sorry, I'm so much better than all of you and I have won! Sorry! Sorry!"

After three hours crowded in the backseat with the board resting on their knees and the rain hammering on the roof and their breath misting up the windows so that they couldn't see out (except where Pippa had dragged her fingers, doodling), they wanted desperately to do anything but play another game. They were, as Pippa had shouted, sick to death of Sorry!

"Stop shouting, stop shouting, stop shouting," Kim was shouting.

"You stop shouting!" Pippa shouted back at her.

"Will you please stop yelling," Kimo yelled. He had slept on the beach and woken before sunrise when the first raindrops had begun to fall.

"I'm not yelling," Pippa yelled.

Toby, who had had enough of it all, crossed his arms over his chest and glared at them. Pierced by

Toby's angry gaze, the others, one by one, stopped yelling. When it was finally quiet—except for the roar of the rain on the car's roof—Kim looked from one to the other and shrugged. "What should we do now?"

It is a funny thing about sunny, tropical islands, but there are very few things to do that don't involve being outdoors, and when it's raining so hard that the raindrops are the size of mushimush berries, trust me, you don't want to be outside. The Fitzgerald-Trouts had been through this often enough that they had a list for just such occasions. Kimo, who was still wearing his wet bathing suit, slid between the seats, plopped into the front one, and opened the glove compartment, pulling out the list.

"Library?"

"Yes," said Kim, crossing her fingers, holding her breath, and staring down the others. She loved the library more than any other place on the island, but they all shook their heads.

"No, no, no."

"Mall?"

"No, no, no, no." It was unanimous. They hated the mall because they didn't ever have enough money to make it fun.

"Movie?"

"Yes, yes, yes," said Kim, Pippa, and Toby. But Kimo said, "Sorry," and this time he meant it. "We went last night. Now we have to save our money for gas until one of the mothers stops by and gives us more." Kimo was in charge of the budget and the others knew not to disagree with him about money. He ran his eye back along the list. "There's only one more thing," he said.

"What is it?" asked Pippa.

"The laundromat," Kimo replied.

And the others shouted, "Yes, yes, yes!"

The children were all wondering why they hadn't thought of going to the laundromat earlier. It was the perfect place to spend a rainy day. For very little money—just a few quarters—they could sit all afternoon in the steamy warmth while their clothes went around and around. There was a vending machine at the laundromat that had been known to malfunction, so sometimes if you banged on the glass with one hand and wriggled the other hand up into the machine, free chocolate bars would drop out. Best of all, there was a little television that hung above the dryers in the laundromat. Mr. Knuckles, the proprietor, was always watching a game show called *Ham!* where contestants filled their mouths with sausages while trying to tell funny jokes. The Fitzgerald-Trout children (like everyone on the island) could not get enough of that show.

While Toby and Pippa put away the Sorry! board, Kim got out of the car in the rain and opened the trunk. She pulled out her stew-can shoes and got back in. She glanced at the to-do list in her pocket:

> *Find a house*
> *Get groceries (also duct tape,*
> *toothpaste, batteries for flashlight)*

*Do laundry*
*Be nicer to Toby*

But to Kim, the first task on the list seemed undoable. She tried not to think about it. Instead, she laced up her stew-can shoes, started the car, and drove off.

No matter how carefully and slowly Kim drove, the car was hard to control in the rain. It slipped and slid on the road and Kim discovered she had to hit the brakes a long time before a stop sign or red light. "I think the tires are wearing down," she whispered to Kimo, who shook his head, not wanting her to say anything in front of the younger children. Kim would have to add "Buy new tires" to her list, but where would they get the money for those?

"We'll have to start taking the bus," piped up Pippa, who had heard Kim.

"We'll figure out something," said Kimo. What

he did not say was that the bus cost money too. A cloud of concern settled over the older two children as Kim pulled the car into the parking lot.

When they'd gathered all the dirty laundry from the corners of the trunk, they raced through the rain toward their favorite place of shelter. Halfway there Pippa shouted, "Look, they've got a new sign!"

It was true, a big new awning hung over the laundromat, and stuck in it were ten large plastic letters that spelled out LAUNDROMAT in a kind of lettering that Pippa had never seen before.

The thing is: Pippa loved fonts. Ever since she had done her first PowerPoint presentation in third grade, she loved to sit at the school computer and type out a word and then try out how it looked in all the different typefaces. She had come to love each font as if it had its own particular character. She loved them so much that she drove her sister and brothers crazy naming the ones she saw on signs. A trip downtown with Pippa sounded like this: "Helvetica, Helvetica, Cambria, Times, Cambria, Chalkduster, Brush Script."

And now here Pippa was in the parking lot of the laundromat facing a font she had never seen before. LAUNDROMAT, the sign said. The word was written in simple block letters but on some of them—the U, the D, the R, the O, and the A's—there were tiny little metal spikes poking up out of the letters. What was the pattern? She shivered in the downpour and watched through rain-splattered glasses as a very wet pigeon flew toward the sign, tried to land, and then flew off. Eureka! she thought. The little spikes were meant to keep the pigeons from landing on certain letters where they could make nests.

While Pippa stood in the rain admiring the sign, the others were already swinging open the door of the laundromat. "Fitzgerald-Trouts," exclaimed Mr. Knuckles as the children shoved into the room. "Lucky day for you! Vending machine broken." Mr. Knuckles didn't own the vending machine and didn't care if the children took as much chocolate as they wanted. He liked them and knew they loved *Ham!* as much as he did.

"Episode start now." He nodded toward the TV. Mr. Knuckles spoke the native language of that island very beautifully, but when he spoke English he left out a lot of words. His sentences were like the roads on the island, full of potholes.

Kimo headed over to bang on the vending machine, and he felt the cloud of concern lifting. It was hard to worry about anything with chocolate and *Ham!* in the works, and the chance to sneak looks at Mr. Knuckles's fabulous tattoos. There were so many interesting, complicated pictures up and down Mr. Knuckles's neck and arms that Kimo could have spent all afternoon just trying to decipher the story they told. Why did Mr. Knuckles have a spaceship tattooed on his arm? And why the word *Mom* on his neck surrounded by a heart with thorns? Did he have a terrible mother too?

Meanwhile Kim had gone to buy a little packet of soap from the dispenser and Toby was over by the cash register saying hello to Goldie. Goldie was a goldfish that Mr. Knuckles had won at a carnival many years before and whose bowl sat on the counter. When Toby tapped on the bowl, Goldie rose to the surface for food, and then Toby was allowed to take a pinch of food from the little canister next to the bowl and feed him. It was the kind of simple, wordless communication that delighted Toby, who could play with Goldie for hours.

As he was sprinkling the food into the bowl for Goldie, Toby noticed a tall cardboard box standing beside the counter. A sign hung over the box, and even though Toby didn't know how to read yet, he knew what it was. There was a slot cut in the top of the box and a pencil taped to a long string that hung from the box and beside the box sat a stack of tickets with a blank line where you could write your name. What else could it be but a contest? There was nothing Toby loved more than a contest.

"Want a bite?" Kimo held a chocolate bar out to Toby, but Toby shrugged it away and nodded toward the box.

"Is that a contest?"

Kimo admitted it was. "Help me enter," said Toby.

"Why would you want to enter?" Kim argued.

"It's a contest," said Toby.

"But why would you want to win a hat tree?" Kim was indignant. Sometimes Toby's stubbornness made her say mean things, things that she regretted later. "You don't wear a hat."

"It's a contest," said Toby.

"There's not enough room for it in the car, even if you did win it."

"It's a contest," Toby said again. He was a boy of few words.

"Watch *Ham!*" said Kimo, trying to turn Toby's attention in a different direction. "That's a contest, and look—it's starting."

Pippa came through the door just then, wiping her glasses on her T-shirt and shouting, "Don't start the laundry! I need to change! My clothes are wet!" Pippa was always shouting because—being the third of four children—she felt she had to. As the oldest, Kim and Kimo got respect; they also got to sit in the two front seats, where they coolly decided the fates of the younger siblings. Toby, as the youngest, got coddled and taken care of. What was left for poor Pippa? If she didn't shout, if she didn't lash out with her stormy temper, no one would pay her the slightest attention—or so it had always seemed to her. Perhaps Pippa was right because Kim, who didn't seem to have heard her, was already tossing the soap into the machine.

"I want to enter the contest," said Toby, tearing a ticket off the stack.

"Anybody enter," said Mr. Knuckles, coming around the counter and patting the box. "No problem. You want enter, you enter. One ticket per customer."

"I want to enter," said Toby.

"Go ahead," said Kimo, giving Kim a look that said *be nice, let him try it*. "But you have to write your own name."

"I'll write his name for him," offered Pippa, still in her wet clothes. "I'll write it in Pigeon font!" She said this last part with excitement in her voice, hoping the others would ask what Pigeon font was, but no one was interested, and anyway the first *Ham!* contestant was smiling as the host of the show set a plate of sausages in front of him.

Kimo turned to the TV. Toby saw that he had given up on making him write his name so he shoved the pencil at Pippa, who took it and began writing Toby's name for him. She drew little spikes in the letters that looked like good spots for a pigeon to build a nest, then she drew a cloud of pigeons circling around his name.

When she was done, Toby took the ticket and blew on it for good luck and crumpled it up a little bit. He thought this gave him a better chance of winning because it made it easier for whoever was drawing the tickets to grab ahold. He pushed the ticket through the box's slot, then he took the chocolate bar that Kimo was holding out to him and joined the others on the plastic chairs in front of the TV set.

He was just taking his first bite of chocolate and watching the *Ham!* contestant take his first bite of sausage when a newscaster appeared on the TV and said, "We interrupt this show with breaking news. The island's top stockbroker has been arrested in a billion-dollar scheme...."

A billion dollars, Toby thought, that's a lot of money! A billion dollars, how many dollar bills is that? How many packets of laundry soap could it buy?

The TV flashed to a picture of a woman wearing curlers and a pair of orange pajamas being led from a house in handcuffs by two police officers.

Toby thought he recognized the lady. He was pretty sure her face was familiar. Hadn't she told him to wash his hands? Hadn't she told him to do his homework? He remembered squinting at her face and thinking: I don't have homework. I'm in kindergarten. And then he remembered he'd been squinting because he could hardly look straight at her. The sunlight reflecting off her diamonds might have blistered his eyes.

Now he turned those eyes to look at Kimo, who nodded as if to say that he was thinking the same thing, just as the two girls said to each other, "Oh no! It's our terrible mother."

CHAPTER
4

"How many dollar bills is a billion dollars?" asked Toby. The four of them were still staring at the TV, watching as Maya Fitzgerald was led to the police car.

"It's a lot of dollar bills," said Kimo. "Truckloads and truckloads."

Kim was staring at the screen with a confused look on her face. "Why is Maya wearing pajamas? It's the afternoon." It was weird to see someone in pajamas in the middle of the day. They made Maya look like she was already in prison. Kim's question hung in the air around them. No one could answer it until Mr. Knuckles piped up from behind the cash register, "Stockbroker work New York hours. Up middle night. Sleep daytime."

What he said sounded true, and if Kim had had any idea what a stockbroker was it might have made sense to her. Mr. Knuckles could see the confused look on Kim's face so he tried to explain that a stockbroker invests people's money through the stock market, which was in New York. Because the island they lived on was in the middle of the ocean and far away from New York, to be a stockbroker you had to get up in the middle of the night and go to bed in the afternoon. If you weren't awake during New York hours, you couldn't be on the Internet trading stocks with all the other stockbrokers. This explained why *that* mother had always looked exhausted when she visited them.

Of course they'd never known what she did for work; she'd been too terribly busy to tell them. But it didn't surprise any of them to find out she had had her hands on truckloads of money. That was how she bought all those diamonds.

"At least her pajamas aren't covered with diamonds," said Pippa. "This is the first time she's actually looked kind of normal."

"It would be hard to sleep wearing diamonds," said practical Kimo.

"Diamond shirts, pants," Mr. Knuckles chimed in, shaking his head, "she broke my dry-cleaning machine. When I tell her she broke it, I ask for money to fix it. She no care. She no help. I never like her, your mother. She one greedy lady."

Now the newscaster was saying exactly that. He was saying that Maya Fitzgerald was accused of using her job as a stockbroker to steal people's money. If it was true, Maya would go to prison for a very long time.

And the thought of that—of Maya in prison—made Kim remember the number one thing on her to-do list. "Hey," she said, "I bet Maya's house is empty."

The other three Fitzgerald-Trouts blinked. What did Kim mean?

"I mean," said Kim, reading their minds, "that if Maya is going to prison, then the house she was living in will be empty." Kim's mind was alive with the exciting thought that they might all soon sleep under a roof.

"It's raining a lot more than it used to," said Kimo, understanding her.

"The tires on the car *are* getting bald." Kim shored up her argument. She and Kimo smiled at each other, feeling that invisible thread that ran between them.

But Toby was shaking his head. He loved the forest near the beach and didn't want to move away from it. Before he could put that feeling into words, Pippa chimed in, "No matter how terrible she is, we can't live in her house without asking."

Kim and Kimo groaned, realizing that Pippa was right.

Just then Mr. Knuckles barked, "She say something." They looked back at the TV and leaned forward in their plastic seats and watched as the police gestured to the reporters to step closer. The reporters rushed toward the car! Cameras flashed! A bouquet of microphones bloomed in front of Maya Fitzgerald.

Maya stepped up to one of the microphones, and this is what she said: "But you can't send me to prison, I have four children to take care of."

That was it. That was all. Then she climbed into the police car and the sirens screamed and the police officers drove her away. The plastic seats squeaked as the Fitzgerald-Trouts sat back in them.

It was Pippa who spoke first. "Four children to take care of? Do we have four brothers and sisters that we don't know about?"

It was what Kimo and Toby were wondering too.

But not Kim. Kim shook her head. "I think she means us."

The other three looked at her incredulously. "Us?"

"Handing your kids a bunch of loose change every few weeks is not taking care of them." Pippa's freckles were flaring with indignation.

"Stopping by their car to tell them to wash their hands isn't taking care of them either." Kimo was indignant too.

"She was too terribly busy to take care of us," snapped Kim.

"And she told me to do my homework when I'm only in kindergarten," offered Toby, a little lamely.

"We've got to do something," said Kim. "If she has the audacity to say she's taking care of us, then we have to be audacious too."

"What are you suggesting?" asked Pippa.

"I don't know yet." Kim took their now clean but very wet clothes out of the washer and put them in a dryer, and then she motioned the others toward the door. "Come on."

They all headed out of the laundromat.

"Wait—" said Mr. Knuckles, but before he could finish, Pippa interrupted. "We know *Ham!* is on, but this is more important."

"No," said Mr. Knuckles. "Contest. Win hat tree. I draw ticket. Five o'clock."

"We'll be back," said Toby, looking at the others with all the sternness a five-year-old can muster when he has chocolate on his nose.

"Yes," said his brother and sisters, because they had to come back anyway when their laundry was dry.

They dashed across the rainy parking lot and climbed into the car to discuss a plan. Kim and Kimo turned around in their seats so that they were facing Pippa and Toby. Kim thought about how the Perfects had a code word for those times when all the children needed to get together to talk about something important; they called it a PS, which stood for Perfect Summit. She briefly imagined trying to come up with a code name for this family meeting. But the truth was, they needed to act quickly, and anyway, Kim thought, what was the point of trying to be like the Perfects when you were posed with a problem so incredibly undignified that no Perfect would ever encounter it? After all, the Fitzgerald-Trout children were meeting to discuss how to take a house away from their mother who was going to jail! It sounded to

Kim like something that might happen to one of the Awfuls, and that thought made her so unhappy that she banished it quickly and brought the meeting to order. "How are we going to get into the jail?" Kim asked abruptly. When no one answered her, she said, "I think we should go to the jail and tell them she's our mother, then demand that they let us see her."

"It won't work," said Toby.

"Why not?" asked Kimo.

"You have to say please," replied Toby. He had been drilled in day care and now in kindergarten on how saying please was the only way to get anything you wanted.

"I don't think just asking and saying please is going to cut it," pronounced Pippa. "We need a better plan than that."

They sat there staring out the windows,

imagining ways they might
reach Maya in her jail cell.
Kim imagined scaling the walls
and Kimo imagined digging
a tunnel. Toby imagined para-
chuting in and Pippa imagined dress-
ing up as a prison guard. None of them said
these ideas out loud. They were too ridiculous.

Finally, into the silence, Toby said, "What if we
say *pretty* please?"

"Unfortunately," snarked Pippa, "that's the
best idea so far."

"Okay, then," said Kim. "Phase One of the
plan is to go to the jail and say 'Can we see our
mother, pretty please?'"

"What's Phase Two?" asked Kimo. "How do
we get Maya to give us the house?"

"Threaten her," Pippa said with relish. "We
have to tell her we're going to go to the TV reporters and we're going to explain how even though

she is dripping with diamonds and has a house the size of...I don't know what, but it must be big... she only ever gave us her spare change."

Kimo and Toby were nodding in agreement, but Kim said, "I don't think so." Kim didn't want Pippa to lose her temper, but she had to disagree with her little sister because she was certain that threatening Maya would never work. Maya was too selfish. If she was threatened, she wouldn't give in; she would try to punish them.

"Maya is terrible," Kim reminded Pippa. "The only way to get her to give us the house is to make her think things are going to be better for her if she does."

Pippa's nose twitched, but she didn't argue.

"Sounds right," Kimo said. "But how is it going to be better for her?"

"I don't know," said Kim. "Let me think about it."

"Think while you drive," said Toby, who

wanted to be back at the laundromat in time for the contest. So Kim put on her stew-can shoes and started the car, and they all set off for the island jail.

On the way to the jail, Kim steered over bumps and holes in the road, peering carefully over the dashboard as they talked about the things that would be different if they had a house. Pippa wanted to take a bath in a real bathtub, and Kimo wanted to sleep in a bed. Kim admitted she had always wanted an oven. An oven? It turned out that Kim cherished a dream of learning to bake. She loved cookies, cakes, and bread—and those are three things you cannot make over a campfire.

As they neared the jail, even Toby was coming around to the idea of a house because he realized that if he won the hat tree he would have a place to put it. Kim parked out front and Kimo used the last of their change—coins Maya had given them— to pay for a parking meter. Then they climbed the large stone steps and pushed open the tall wooden doors to talk to the jailer who was on duty.

"We'd like to see our mother, Maya Fitzgerald," Kim said. The other three added in unison, "Pretty please."

To their utter surprise, the jailer nodded. "It's island policy to let jailed parents have a visit with their children."

"Man, I love this island!" Kimo whispered to the others as they were guided by the jailer down a long hallway and then whisked into a big, heavy, iron-doored elevator that lowered them down into the basement, where the jail cells were.

"Hello, children," said Maya as the jailer ushered the four Fitzgerald-Trouts into the tiny cell and swung the doors shut behind them. "Don't touch the…" Maya scolded, but it was too late. The children were already climbing all over the cell. They had never been in a jail before, but like most people they had imagined being in one, and so the second they stepped inside they wanted to try out what it was like to be a prisoner. Toby had his leg halfway out and was spitting on the bars to make them slippery enough to slide through. Kimo was up on the bunk. Kim was shaking the bars, saying, "Set me free, set me free." Little Pippa was down on her knees with her pencil, making marks on the floor like a prisoner tallying up her days behind bars.

Maya stamped her foot. "Stop it right now! Do you know where those metal bars have been? Go wash!"

Luckily there was a little sink in the jail cell. (There was also a very small, very low toilet with absolutely no seat.) They took turns washing their hands, and when they were done they sat in a row on the bunk. Maya was pacing the cell, waiting for a call from her lawyer. "Why are you here?" she asked. "I'm terribly busy and I'm terribly tired." Kim wanted to say she was tired of the mother being terrible, but she knew better than to get in an argument when she was there to ask for a house.

"We were thinking…" said Kim, trailing off and looking at Pippa. Now that Kim was faced with her pacing mother, she wasn't so sure she was right about her strategy. Maybe they should do as Pippa had suggested and threaten Maya.

"What?" asked the mother, who could hardly keep her eyelids open. "What were you thinking? Get on with it!"

"We were thinking," Kim tried again, and Pippa nodded at her, encouraging. "Since you're in jail, maybe you would like someone—or someones—to look after your house." Then, as if on cue, the other three children beamed big, toothy smiles to make it clear to this mother that they were the someones Kim was talking about.

"Oh," said the mother, blinking in her sleepiness. "But what about the car?"

"We would park it in the driveway," said Kim, encouraged that she hadn't been given an outright no.

"Don't you like living in it?" the mother said. "Fitzgerald always said you did."

"Are you nuts?" Pippa yelped, jumping to her feet and putting her hands on her hips. The mother blinked as if the words had struck her in the face. Kim grinned, pleased to see Pippa's temper put to good use. "We didn't like it! We used microscopes as pillows."

"Oh," said the mother.

"We don't all fit," Kimo added.

"We're stacked on top of each other," said Kim.

"I don't want to leave the forest," said Toby.

Kim was shaking her head, wishing Toby, who never spoke, had never spoken. "Don't worry, Toby, if you miss the forest you can always visit."

"Well," said the mother, "I don't know..." Her

mouth flopped open. She seemed to be trying to think of a way to say no. But she was so terribly tired that she couldn't come up with one. She just stood there with her mouth open. Kimo said later that standing there in her pajamas with her puffy eyes and her mouth like that, she looked like an orange sea bass hooked on a fishing line and reeled up out of the water. They had caught her.

"Is that a yes?" Kim nervously asked, and all the children held their breath, wondering if that night they might sleep under a roof.

"You'd have to water the plants," the mother said.

They nodded.

"And vacuum the rugs."

They nodded again.

"And wash the windows."

More nods.

"When a house gets dirty, you can't just drive it through the car wash," she finished.

Kim shot Pippa a look, begging her not to say anything. "Is that a yes?"

Blinking and nodding, Maya said, "Well, I suppose so."

Silence fell over the tiny jail cell. You could have heard a jailhouse mouse squeak. The four Fitzgerald-Trout children were stunned by this turn of events. A house! A house! A house!

Kim thought about how she had a catalog from the Swiss furniture store MARRA stashed in the trunk of the car. On weekends, while the others were swimming, she would sometimes take it out and lie on the beach paging through it and imagining living in a house filled with that furniture. Now, standing in the jail cell, she realized she was finally going to be able to take that catalog out of the car and put it on a shelf in Maya's house. Maybe someday she was even going to be able to order some of that Swiss furniture.

"How big is the house?" she asked.

Maya shrugged, then almost absentmindedly began to count the rooms on her fingers. "Living room, dining room, parlor, kitchen, study, six

bedrooms, no, I think it's seven…" She was well out of fingers but she was still counting. "…four bathrooms. Then, of course, there's the guesthouse and the swimming pool."

"There's a pool?" Kimo asked.

"And a hot tub," said Maya.

It was unimaginable.

But Pippa didn't seem pleased. She was squinching up her face and the freckles on her cheeks were darkening. "You had this enormous house and you never invited us?" She spit out the question.

Kim shrank back, but Maya just blinked and shrugged. "I was too busy for guests."

"Guests?" Pippa shouted. "Most people don't think of their children as guests!"

Maya blinked again and Kim was suddenly terrified that she might change her mind. "It sounds magnificent," Kim hurriedly said. "And we'll take great care of it. We just need the keys—"

"And the address," said Kimo.

"Right, yes, of course, I'll get them for you—" But Maya was interrupted by a sharp, piercing sound. It was her phone. She put it to her ear. "Yes," she said, then in a graver voice, "No, no, no, no. Oh no."

She hung up with a gasp. "That was my lawyer," she said, and slumped down onto the bunk beside them, her head hanging, her mouth in a frown.

"What is it?" Kim asked. "Is everything all right?"

A tear was rolling down Maya's cheek. For a full minute no one spoke and then at last Maya said, "He called to say that the police came."

"The police?" Kimo shook his head. "But you're already in jail."

"No," Maya explained, "they came to my place. They took all my diamonds and they took all my furniture...." She trailed off, shaking her head like it was all just a bad dream.

"Is that all?" asked Kim.

"No," said Maya. "They took the house."

"Took your house?" Kim asked in a quavering voice. "How?"

"They locked the windows and sealed the doors. They're selling it off to pay my debts."

Maya hung her head again and for a moment the children almost felt sorry for her. But not really. They couldn't. They were too sorry for themselves. The house with the living room, dining room, parlor, kitchen, study, six (or seven) bedrooms, four bathrooms, guesthouse, pool, and hot tub was not going to be theirs. Kim thought about the MARRA catalog stashed in the trunk of the car. It was going to be there a while longer.

And then something unbelievable happened. Maya looked up at the four Fitzgerald-Trout children and said, "I've been a terrible mother."

Kim, Kimo, and Toby didn't say anything. But Pippa couldn't help herself. Scowling and adjusting her glasses on her nose, she said, "You were an even worse stockbroker," and then she let loose her terrifying laugh.

CHAPTER
6

They drove back to the laundromat in silence. What was there to say? They had come so close to getting a house. But their dream had been snatched away. It wasn't just that things were as bad as they had been the night before when they realized they didn't fit in the car; things were much worse. However much they hated the visits from the terrible mothers, they had been a source of money for gas and other things. Now they knew it would be a long time before they saw any more loose change from Maya Fitzgerald.

By the time they reached the parking lot of the laundromat, the rain had stopped. There was water everywhere and the oil dripping from all the parked cars made wild rainbows that spread around their feet as the Fitzgerald-Trouts stomped in those puddles. Kim was thinking how one of the best things about not having parents was that no one told you not to stomp in the puddles, and no one told you not to splash your brothers and sister when you did. Stomping and splashing made Kim think how amazing it was that something as ugly as gasoline could make something as beautiful as a rainbow if you splashed the water just right. The thought cheered her up a little.

The bells tinkled and Mr. Knuckles looked up as they pushed open the door. He was standing over the cardboard box surrounded by four or five other laundromat customers: an old man with an eye patch dressed in a heavy sailor's coat, a very tall woman who was wearing a tutu, a husband and wife who were nervously leaning into each other, and a postal worker. It was hard to tell if the postal worker was there for the contest or just dropping off the mail, but he was watching Mr. Knuckles, who was shaking the box with all the tickets in it. Beside him, the shiny new hat tree stood, waiting for its lucky new owner. Heading toward the dryers to get their clothes, Kim recognized the hat tree from the MARRA catalog. For a second she hoped that Toby would win it, but then she realized how ridiculous this was. Where would they ever put a hat tree?

"Here we go," Mr. Knuckles announced without much ceremony, then he took the lid off the box, closed his eyes, and reached his hand down inside. Toby could picture Mr. Knuckles's fingers (and his knuckles) bumping up against his crumpled raffle ticket. Mr. Knuckles was sure to feel the shape and grab ahold of an edge. It was much easier than picking up an uncrumpled ticket, Toby thought, and he found himself silently saying, Plucky knucky make me lucky, plucky knucky make me lucky, plucky knucky make me lucky.... He had no idea where it had come from, but there it was, unspooling in his mind.

After what seemed to Toby a very long time, Mr. Knuckles finally pulled the winning ticket up out of the box. Immediately Toby felt his heart sink. He could see that the winning ticket was not crumpled and unless someone had ironed out all the tickets while they were in the box (something that, he supposed, could happen in a laundromat), he could not possibly have won. But he held his breath anyway. And he was still holding it when Mr. Knuckles unfolded the ticket and read the name: "Keiko Okada." The tall woman in the tutu jumped up and down. Mr. Knuckles handed her the hat tree. She took it in her arms and danced around with it so that for a minute the hat tree looked like her ballet partner. "I've never won anything in my life!" she said, and Toby tried to feel happy for her. But he could not and neither could the rest of the small crowd, who were all dispersing, banging on the vending machine one last time and gathering their baskets of laundry.

Kimo put his big arms around Toby. "It's okay," he said. "It wouldn't have fit in the car anyway."

Pippa punched Toby in the shoulder (softly in that nice way that sisters sometimes do) and said, "You'll win next time." Then Kim came over carrying their folded laundry and hugged him. "I'm sorry," she said, biting her lip and fighting the helpless, sinking feeling that there was nothing she could do to make her little brother feel better. Toby just shrugged and looked away. He wasn't going to let himself cry, but it was really, really hard not to.

It had been an awful day for the Fitzgerald-Trout children. Watching from the register, Mr. Knuckles saw this. He knew, of course, what had happened to terrible Maya, and he could guess from the look on Kim's face when they came in that the visit at the jail had not gone well, and now to see the littlest Fitzgerald-Trout trying not to cry with that tiny bit of chocolate dried to his nose was more than Mr. Knuckles could stand. "Toby," he called out. When Toby turned around, Mr. Knuckles said, "I draw one more. Second place." He walked toward the box.

"But you don't have another hat tree," said Toby.

"I better prize," said Mr. Knuckles. "Close eyes."

Toby did as he was told and closed his eyes. Mr. Knuckles reached into that box and lifted out all the raffle tickets, reading them one by one. Finally he found Toby's.

"Winner!" he said. "Open eyes." As Toby opened his eyes, Mr. Knuckles read out, "Toby Fitzgerald-Trout."

A smile burst across Toby's face like the sun through clouds. "I won?" He couldn't believe it. "What did I win?"

Mr. Knuckles ran his eye around the laundromat looking for something, anything that could be a prize. At last he saw it. He walked over to the counter and picked up Goldie's bowl. "Second prize," he said, handing Goldie to Toby, whose eyes were as wide and bright as the goldfish's bowl. Then strongman Kimo scooped Toby up and lifted him onto his shoulder. Pippa shouted, "Hurrah! Hurrah!"—because why not? She wanted some fun too—and Kimo paraded Toby around the laundromat. The goldfish bowl sloshed water as Toby clutched it proudly to his chest.

"Thank you, Mr. Knuckles," Kim whispered. "Thank you."

K im's feeling of gratitude didn't last very long.
By the time they'd driven back to the parking lot at the beach, Kim and Pippa were cursing
Mr. Knuckles's name. (Kimo probably would have
too, but he wasn't the kind to curse anyone.) Twice
on the way home they had nearly killed Goldie
when the water from his bowl had sloshed, and
those same two times they'd had to make emergency stops at a gas station to refill the bowl. How
could Mr. Knuckles have given them a goldfish

when they lived in a car on an island covered with bumpy roads?

That night they couldn't sleep on the beach because the sand was too wet and Kim was certain that if they did they would catch terrible colds. Pippa didn't agree with her, and she told her so, saying that she sounded like one of the terrible mothers, but Kim put her foot down. So as the moon rose over the beach, the children climbed into the car. Kim and Kimo got in the front with their seats tilted back as far as they would go. Pippa and Toby tried sleeping with their heads at different ends of the backseat. It meant they might kick each other in the face, but they did seem to fit better.

"What about Goldie?" Toby asked.

"Can't he sleep back there with you?" said Kim.

"If we put him on the floor one of us might fall on him and knock over his bowl," said Pippa. "Why don't you put him on the floor up front?"

"He'll get knocked over by our feet," said Kim.

"I guess it's the dashboard," offered Kimo. So Toby passed up the bowl, which was placed on the dashboard next to the alarm clock that Kim set every night so that they could get up in time for school.

The misery of fish ownership only got worse over the next few days. They took turns holding the bowl when they were driving, but it sloshed and splashed and had to be refilled every few blocks. The mood in the car was always tense. At night they kept the bowl on the dashboard, but in the morning they sometimes forgot it was there, and Kim would drive off and the bowl would go flying, launching Goldie into the air. He would flip and flop around the car, all of them screaming at one another to be careful and not squash him. All of them trying to catch him or scoop him up from under their feet.

It was awful! And poor Goldie! After many peaceful years in the laundromat watching episodes of *Ham!* and listening to the chime of the cash register, what must Goldie have thought of his dangerous new life? Pippa said that she thought Goldie looked outraged—like the angry fish she'd seen drawn in a Dr. Seuss book. This made Toby furious and he kicked her very hard. She kicked him back. And next thing you know, the two of them were thrashing around in the backseat, punching and kicking and tugging on each other's hair. It was not the Fitzgerald-Trout children's finest hour, and Kim knew that something had to change.

But what? She could not get rid of the fish. Toby would be heartbroken, and he would certainly never forgive her. The only solution was obvious and was the number one thing on the to-do list in the notebook in her pocket, but she had still not figured out how to get it done.

The morning after Pippa and Toby's fight was another school day so the Fitzgerald-Trouts ate breakfast at the beach, brushed their teeth in the public bathroom, and then dutifully headed to school, where they parked in a shady corner of the parking lot, left Goldie in his bowl on the dashboard, and got out of the car. Toby had a bruise on his cheek where Pippa had hit him and Pippa had a sore spot where he had ripped her hair out, but otherwise, walking in bare feet and carrying brown paper lunch bags, they looked just like every other group of children heading to class.

"Chit, please," Toby said to Kim. He was talking about one of the little slips of paper they were given at the beginning of each month so that each day they could get a free milk from the school at lunchtime. Kim reached into her pocket and pulled out the little notebook, where the chits were folded at the back. She handed them around to the others and then watched as Toby ran off to see a group of his friends who were gathered under the tallest tree in the yard. The other Fitzgerald-Trouts knew what Toby was going to do; it was something they had all done when they were his age. He was going to gamble his milk chit.

What none of the architects of Windward School could possibly have imagined when they built the school so many years ago was that they had built a place perfectly designed to encourage gambling. They had built the school in the middle of a big grass lawn and they had built it without any walls. Because the island's weather was always warm, each classroom was just a square concrete floor with a column at all four corners holding up a thatched roof. Under the roof sat rows of chairs and desks, and at the front was a free-standing chalkboard. What none of the architects anticipated was that because the classrooms were open to the air, birds would come and go as they pleased, and because the lawn was surrounded by mushimush trees, the birds would carry berries in their beaks. This had the perfect makings of a game. Every morning before school, the younger children met beneath the biggest tree to bet their milk chits on who would be the first child that day to get a mushimush berry dropped on his or her head by one of those birds. It was terrifically embarrassing to have a mushimush berry crack open and splatter all over you—and if it was the first of the morning, then a small cheer would go up from those who'd bet on you and a groan from those who had lost. It put a lot of excitement into the school morning and had the added benefit of driving the teachers crazy.

The game had been going on for as long as any of the Fitzgerald-Trouts could remember, but what none of them knew was that the game had been invented by Kimo's father, Johnny Trout. It was Johnny who had first stood under the tallest tree and watched a bird fly off with a berry and thought up the wager. After that, he was the one who stood under the tree every morning taking bets. As I remember it, Johnny never placed a bet himself; instead he kept a small portion of the winner's earnings. He wasn't a mean boy; he

always gave some of his winnings to whatever child had had that first berry dropped on his or her head. That was still the tradition. In fact, some children (who didn't mind being splattered) hoped they would get the berry to the head.

That morning Toby placed his bet, then went off to the kindergarten classroom. Kim was taking a seat at her desk in her classroom. It was a geometry lesson and the teacher told them to get out their protractors. Kim did as she was told and soon was drawing circles with the instrument. But it was hard to concentrate. Every circle she drew made her think of Goldie's bowl and its fragile inhabitant floating above the car's dashboard. In other words, every circle made Kim think about their desperate need for a house. Now the teacher was telling them to draw a thirty-degree angle, and as Kim did, she let herself imagine going to one of the terrible mothers for help. She knew she

couldn't talk to terrible Maya, who was still in jail. But what about terrible Tina?

Tina was a country-and-western singer whose most recent song was steadily climbing the pop-music charts. Maybe, Kim thought, when Tina shows up with the monthly envelope of money, I can ask for her advice about a house. But then Kim remembered how the last few months Tina hadn't actually delivered the money herself. She had sent her boyfriend to deliver it. Kim didn't know his name, but she remembered he wore a blue tuxedo and drove a matching blue convertible.

Kim supposed that if she wanted help she should start by going to find Tina at her recording studio. But then Kim pictured Tina surrounded by her gold and platinum CDs mounted like trophies on the walls. Tina would be smiling and pretending to listen to Kim's troubles while she checked her reflection in those shiny discs. Ugh, Kim thought, I would rather give up my seat and sleep curled up in the trunk than ask for Tina's help.

The buzzer sounded for recess and silently Kim joined the throng of shouting children who were running toward the playground. As she emerged onto the lawn, she could see Pippa already crouched down in the dirt drawing some diagram while she talked to someone. She's probably explaining our family tree to a new friend, thought Kim. And there was Toby, hanging upside down from the monkey bars, his T-shirt falling over his head. He must not have won the mushimush bet or he would be counting his winnings. And there was Kimo, dashing out to the middle of the field to play football with a group of other kids. What's wrong with me? thought Kim. Why can't I just have fun? Because I'm the one who learned how to drive when I was eight years old. That's why. It makes me responsible for everyone. That thought made her feel very alone.

She could see the car sitting there in the school parking lot on the other side of the row of mushimush trees. *The Perfects* was under her seat in the car. She decided to go and get it so that she could read during recess. What she needed was to fall into the happy world of the Perfects, where the most terrible thing that could happen was having your dog trample your poster the morning of the science fair. But this thought led Kim to a surprising discovery: She realized she was a little tired of the Perfects and their just-so-perfect world. It was so unlike her own.

When Kim got to the car, she found herself going to the trunk and taking out her MARRA catalog instead. Something—perhaps it had been the conversation with Maya in the jail cell—made her want to take a peek at all that furniture.

The catalog was thick and it took her almost the whole recess to get through it. She leafed through dozens and dozens of pages, staring at hundreds and hundreds of pieces of furniture and reading their Swiss names out loud to Goldie, who was sitting on the dashboard. There were as many names in the catalog as there were children playing on the playground. Kim was sure the furniture was just as friendly. "If we had a house," she told Goldie, "each of us would have our own bed and desk, and we could put you on a shelf." She flipped through the catalog and found a photograph of a bright blue bookshelf named Slawz. "You could sit on Slawz all day," she said, tapping Goldie's bowl. "I bet you'd become friends." Then she sighed an unhappy sigh, thinking of all the obstacles that stood in the way of Goldie's friendship with the blue bookshelf.

Just as Kim was turning the last page of the catalog, the recess buzzer rang. "Bye, Goldie," she said, climbing out of the car. "Maybe some afternoon we'll go to MARRA to see all that furniture." Just saying this out loud made her think how much it would lift her spirits to go to MARRA. After all, the store wasn't far. It was right downtown. Why not visit? And then, as Kim closed the trunk, she had an even better idea.

CHAPTER
8

The first thing that struck Kim when they walked into MARRA was how enormous it was. It was so big that the whole of their school, including the wide field that surrounded the pavilions, could have fit inside it. And that was just the first floor. As Kimo pointed out, there were stairs, right at the entrance, leading up to a second floor that he wagered must be just as large.

"It makes sense that it's this big," said Kim. "It

has to fit all that furniture from all those pages in the catalog."

Toby was tugging on Kim's sleeve. "I have to pee," he said. So that was the second thing that struck Kim: A little brother is annoying wherever you are, even when you are in the store of your dreams.

"Why didn't you pee before we got here?" she asked.

"I didn't have to till now," said Toby, who was moving from one foot to the other. Kimo saw how uncomfortable Toby was and took Goldie's bowl from him. "We'll find a bathroom somewhere," he said.

Kim was already moving farther into the building. There was a yellow line on the floor and there were signs telling you to follow it. The children did as they were told and quickly discovered that the store was laid out as a series of rooms. Each room displayed the furniture from the MARRA catalog. The rooms didn't have full walls or ceilings but

were arranged to look like they could be lived in. There were several bedrooms and each one had a bed made up with sheets and blankets. Each had a rug. Each had a bedside table with a lamp. Each had a bookshelf with books. There were dining rooms that had tables and chairs, and on every table there was a bowl full of clam cutlets with little toothpicks stuck in them.

MARRA was famous for these cutlets, which were sold in the food section. Walking past them, the children found the smell irresistible. They bent over one of the bowls, sniffing, then poking gently, then finally stuffing the little balls of fried clam into their open mouths. They gorged on those free clam cutlets until Kimo realized that people were beginning to stare.

"We have to blend in," he said, scooting the

others back into the crowd of people who were following the yellow line to the kitchen section. Though the kitchens didn't have running water, they had all the gadgets. Kim was admiring the mixer and blender and toaster when Toby tugged on her hand again. "I have to pee."

"Okay," she said. They headed back to the yellow line, which led them to the bathroom section of the store. Toby was about to pull shut a sliding door to one of the model bathrooms when Pippa yanked his hand and said, "Don't!"

"But I have to," whined Toby.

"That's not a real bathroom," Pippa said. "It doesn't have pipes." Sure enough, this bathroom was just another part of the display.

"Oh," said Toby, chastened. "But where's the real one? I need it."

"We're looking," said Pippa, rolling her eyes at Kim. Why did Toby have to make everything so difficult?

They were hurrying now, actively looking

for a bathroom while Kim rattled off the Swiss names of the pieces of furniture they passed. All the while she was thinking how brilliant her idea had been. If it worked, they would be sleeping in MARRA beds that night—and maybe every night from now on. All they had to do was hide while the MARRA store was closing up and then stay in their hiding places while the MARRA security guards searched the place. Once the guards had gone home for the night, the children could emerge from their hiding spots and find a bed to sleep in. Now that Kim saw how the store was organized, she realized they would not find just a bed to sleep in. In fact, they could each choose a whole bed-room. Imagine!

"How much farther?" Toby wailed.

"We're almost there," said Kim, who wasn't sure where they were but needed Toby to hold it a while longer. "Let's try this way." She stepped off the yellow path and darted between a couple of rooms.

"Weren't we here once already?" Kimo asked as they passed a bedroom with a green bed and a leafy carpet.

"We went in a loop," said Pippa.

"Noooo," Toby whined. "I can't hold it."

"We're going to find it," said Kim. "It's got to be this way. Try to think about something else," she added. Then, "Everybody gets to pick their own room for the night. What room do you guys want?"

"I want the yellow room," said Pippa. She meant the room with the yellow desk and the high yellow canopy bed. There was a wicker toy basket and she had already determined that it would make a good hiding spot.

"What about you, Toby?" Kimo asked.

Toby stopped thinking about having to pee long enough to say that he wanted the green room they had just passed. There was a telescope set up in one corner (not that you could see the stars, but the idea was cool) and there was a shelf where he could set Goldie's bowl.

Kimo decided he wanted a room furnished in brown with a brown leather love seat. Across from it stood a bathroom with a dark shower curtain he could hide behind when the time came.

Kim was just about to say that she wanted the blue room when a computerized voice came on over the loudspeakers. "Two minutes to closing time. All MARRA customers must exit now."

"Oh no," said Kim. "I'm sorry, Toby."

"But I need the bathroom." Toby was emphatic. "Please..."

Kim felt their dream slipping away, and Kimo must have too because he kneeled down and looked Toby in the eye. "Can't you hold it—just for a little bit longer?"

Toby sucked in his lower lip and nodded gravely, then he took back Goldie's bowl.

While the other customers swept past them heading for the exits, the children darted back to their chosen rooms with their chosen hiding spots.

Kim watched where each of them went so that later she would be able to find them.

Toby set Goldie's bowl on a shelf and then slid under the green bed. Pippa opened the lid of the wicker toy basket and climbed inside, lowering herself and then lowering the lid. Kimo ducked into the shower and pulled the dark shower curtain across the rod. Then Kim opened the doors of a tall wooden wardrobe and climbed into that.

Really what they were doing was just playing an enormous game of hide-and-seek, only they hoped that no one would seek them. Now all they had to do was wait and see. And Toby had to wait and not pee.

Just as Kim had predicted, a few minutes after hiding, they heard the idle whistling of a security guard heading through the building. Kim cracked open the door of the wardrobe and peeked out. She could see that he was following the yellow line and glancing into each of the rooms to make sure no customers were left. He swept toward Kim and she could hear the walkie-talkie on his hip squawking. He cleared her room and headed toward the green one, where Toby was hiding under the bed. Through the open sliver of the wardrobe door, Kim could see him. Poor thing, she thought.

Kim held her breath, waiting for the guard to move past Toby, but as he arrived at the green room, the guard stopped.

Under the bed, his heart racing, Toby could see the guard's shoes only a few feet away. The shoes started forward. Only this time not on the yellow line. From their different spots, Kim and Toby both saw that the guard was walking toward Goldie's bowl on the shelf. Perhaps the guard had seen the goldfish and sensed that something was amiss?

The guard tapped on the glass bowl. Goldie rose to the surface, as if it were time for him to be fed. The guard looked at the fish. The fish looked at the guard. Kim's heart was in her throat and Toby, under the bed, was trying desperately not to make a sound.

Then the guard shrugged and stepped back, turning and heading for the yellow line. Phew, thought Kim, in her wardrobe. Double phew, thought Toby, under the bed. But it wasn't over yet because just as the guard was stepping out of the room, he stumbled.

From under the bed, Toby could see what had made him stumble. The guard's shoelace was untied. Toby squeezed as far back under the bed as he could just as the guard bent over to tie his shoe. He hadn't seen Toby yet, but if he turned his head even an inch, he would. Just as Toby was thinking that he would most certainly be caught, an even more terrible thing happened.

A clam cutlet fell out of the security guard's pocket.

It hit the floor with a thunk.

Do you know what happens to a five-year-old when a clam cutlet falls out of someone's pocket?

I'll tell you what happens. The five-year-old laughs.

The laugh rose up out of Toby's belly. But Toby must have felt it rising, because he snapped his mouth shut and swallowed. This only managed to trap the laugh between his ribs and his throat. It hung there, trying to find a way out, trying to squeeze past Toby's lips. Toby pressed them shut. He was holding himself in the necessary place so that he wouldn't pee in his pants. But oh, how that laugh wanted out. It tried to come out Toby's nose. It tried tickling his throat and tickling his ribs.

Toby held on. His ribs ached, his throat ached, not to mention his full bladder. That laugh was doing everything it could to make Toby explode. His face was turning red. His eyes were crossed. Now he had to go to the bathroom really, really badly.

But Toby held on, and finally—it seemed to him like a hundred years later—the security guard picked up the clam cutlet, popped it into his mouth, and moved on down the yellow line.

Toby let out his breath in a long gasp.

Kim, in her wardrobe, let hers out too. She had seen and heard the whole thing.

They stayed in their hiding places for a few minutes longer until the lights in the store clicked off. Taking that as a good sign, Kim stepped out of the wardrobe and called quietly to the others, "We did it." Kimo, who had the flashlight, grabbed Toby and hoisted him over his shoulder, carrying him off to find a real bathroom.

Later, they gathered in one of the dining rooms to eat the fish sandwiches that Kim had brought in her backpack. They'd turned on the lamps now that the guard had gone.

"It wasn't too bad," said Pippa.

"I almost got caught," said Toby, who was feeling fine now that he had used the toilet.

"But you didn't," said Kim, licking butter off her fingers.

"Here," Pippa said, shoving a napkin at her.

Kim studied it with delight. A napkin, a folded

piece of cloth. How wonderful. Usually they used their T-shirts to wipe their hands. "What else can we use?" Kim asked.

"Plates," said Pippa.

"We're almost done eating," said Kimo.

"Who cares?" Pippa jumped to her feet and got plates from the cupboard, handing them out to the others along with silverware that they definitely didn't need.

Kimo used the knife and fork to cut the rest of his sandwich. "Jolly good," he said with his terrible British accent.

As soon as they were done, Pippa got up. "Give me the flashlight. I'll do the dishes."

"Me too," cried Toby, scrambling to join her. They headed to a sink in one of the kitchens, then remembered there was no water. They pretended to wash until they got bored, then they stashed the dirty dishes under the sink.

By the light of the flashlight, they made their way along the yellow line until they found Kim and Kimo sitting on a couch in one of the living rooms pretending to watch a cardboard TV that had a drawing of a weather map on its screen. Kimo fiddled with the remote control. "You always want to watch the weather!" Kim complained. "Let's watch something else." They'd seen this kind of behavior in movies and knew how to play their roles.

"If I want to watch the weather, I will!" Kimo said gruffly.

"What's on?" Pippa asked.

"Kimo just wants to watch the weather," said Kim.

"Boring," said Toby. "How about *Ham!*"

The drawing of the weather map might have been boring, but arguing over TV was not. They went on snarking and sniping and grouching with one another in a pretend way until it was time for lights-out. That was when Pippa did something that surprised them all. She turned to Kim and said, "Will you tuck me in?"

"Tuck you in?" It came out sounding meaner than Kim had meant it. She was just surprised. Tucking in was the kind of thing that parents did and none of them had ever wanted parents.

"Forget it!" Pippa snapped.

"No, it's okay, I'm sorry," said Kim. "Come on, let's find your room." Kim got up and Pippa didn't argue. She followed Kim back to the yellow line, turning to Toby and Kimo and saying, "Night."

"Night," they said.

Once in the yellow room, Pippa put on the T-shirt she slept in while Kim pulled back the covers on the bed. Kim was feeling bad about having been mean, and noticing—for the first time in a long time—how small and fragile Pippa looked in her long T-shirt. It had once belonged to Kim and had several holes. "Ready?"

Pippa nodded and climbed under the sheets, taking off her glasses and setting them on a bedside table. Kim pulled the blanket up around her (as the Perfect mother in the storybook did).

"Good night," she said. Then she remembered and said, "Dear."

"Night," said Pippa as Kim switched off the lamp and started out of the room. "This bed is as big as the moon," she added drowsily, already collapsing into her dreams.

Kim walked back to her room, thinking how exciting it would be to do her homework at a real and actual desk. She could spread her books out. She could press down hard with her pen. And when she was done she could stay up as long as she wanted, reading a book in bed.

Kimo, in his room, was doing push-ups. He could do 527 without stopping, but tonight he was going to see if he could break that record. After all, doing push-ups on a brown shag carpet had to be easier than doing push-ups in a parking lot.

Toby, for his part, sat in his room playing with the telescope. There were no windows and so he couldn't see any stars, but that didn't stop him. He peered through the telescope's lens and played with the knobs and tried to bring the light of the bright red EMERGENCY EXIT sign into focus. Thrilling as this was, he found after a few minutes that his eyes would not stay open. He climbed into the bed and pulled back the covers and then a strange thing happened. His room was suddenly completely bright, as if the sun had risen. He looked up and saw that the overhead lights in the store had all come on, and other lights were coming on too. Red lights flashed down from the ceiling. What was happening?

"Kim?" Toby warbled, stumbling from his bed toward the yellow line just as an alarm began to shriek from somewhere near the door. Before Toby could even react, the computerized voice came over the loudspeaker again, only this time it sounded like it was shouting. *"Security breach! Security breach!"* Toby was running back along the yellow line now, shouting, *"Kim! Kimo! Pippa!"*

The other children were stumbling, sleepy-eyed, from their rooms. Kim's face looked stricken, as if she'd been betrayed by a friend. But she was shouting, *"Run! Run!"*

So they did, racing down the yellow line toward the store's exit. Just as they reached the cash registers, Toby stopped in his tracks. "I left Goldie!" he cried.

"You can't go back," said Kimo. "The police might be coming."

"I have to," Toby pleaded.

"You can't!" Kim confirmed, grabbing him by the hand and tugging him toward the exit. She was terrified that the doors would be locked tight and they would be trapped inside the store until the police came. But when she reached the large metal door and slammed her weight against it, it sprang open.

With relief, the Fitzgerald-Trouts fled into the starry night.

CHAPTER
9

Kim spent the night on the beach lying awake in the sand, imagining the next morning when they had to go back to the MARRA store to get Goldie. She thought how the whole incident must have been filmed and she was sure some security guard would recognize them and drag them off to jail. She could see the newspaper headlines now: TERRIBLE MOTHER SHARES JAIL CELL WITH TERRIBLE CHILDREN.

Still, they had to get Goldie. It was on the top

of her to-do list. Who would feed the goldfish if they didn't? Kim was wondering this as she set out the bowls for cereal and Kimo got the cooler out of the trunk. The ice in the cooler was melted again and the milk for the cereal was starting to get warm. Kim added that to her list:

> *Get Goldie*
> *Find house*
> *Buy fishing line*
> *Give Pippa and Toby haircuts*
> *Ice for cooler*
> *Milk*

They ate around the campfire in silence, and when they were done, Kim said, "Let's go get Goldie."

"Are you nuts?" Kimo asked. Apparently he had no intention of rescuing the fish.

"But we can't leave him there," whimpered Toby. "He'll miss me."

"I'm sorry," challenged Kimo. "We can't risk going back."

"My backpack is there," said Pippa. "And my glasses." So that settled it. They drove in silence back to MARRA and were standing outside as the doors opened.

Kim shoved her hands into her pockets so that the other children wouldn't see that they were trembling with worry. But as the Fitzgerald-Trouts passed through the doors, no security guard stopped them and none of the salesclerks seemed to recognize them either. They found Goldie sitting on the shelf just where Toby had left him.

If there is a contented look that goldfish have, Goldie had that look, and as Toby snatched him from his perch, Kimo couldn't help thinking that the fish would be happier if he were left where he was.

Pippa found her backpack and her glasses. Then they hurried toward the exit and shoved through the doors as quickly as they could. They didn't want to be late for school. It was only a few days until spring break and all the schoolchildren on the island were making origami frogs in bright colors to give to their families and friends. It was an old island custom celebrating the coming of spring.

But it turned out that the Fitzgerald-Trouts weren't going to be folding any paper frogs that morning. The tire that had been so bald a few days before was even balder now and the road between MARRA and the school was filled with potholes. A bald tire and a pothole are not a good combination. Add to it a family of puk-puk geese ambling across the road, and I for one was not surprised to hear what happened next....

As Kim rounded a corner, Kimo shouted, "Look out!" There were the geese in the middle of the road. Kim saw them and swerved to avoid them, but when she did, the bald tire hit the pothole the wrong way.

*Boom!* The tire burst and the car zigzagged out of control.

What happened then happened very slowly.

Kimo said it was like watching a wave form in the ocean. He could see the car spin away from the geese and toward the thick field of sugarcane that grew just beyond the shoulder of the road. He heard Pippa shout from the backseat, "Whoa!" Then he heard Toby wail, "Noooooooo!"

The pothole had launched Goldie out of his bowl and he was flying toward the windshield. Kimo reached out and snatched the fish from the air, catching Goldie between his cupped hands. He turned to look at Kim. She was gritting her teeth and clenching the steering wheel and pressing her stew-can shoes down on the brake.

Slowly, slowly, slowly—or so it seemed to Kimo—Kim guided the car away from the geese and brought it onto the dirt shoulder beside the road, where it stirred up a cloud of dust before finally coming to a stop.

The car was facing backward and the tire was popped, but everyone was unharmed. Or were they?

Toby was crying, "Where is he? Where is he?" He scrambled into the front seat.

"In here," said Kimo, nodding toward his hands, which were gripped tightly shut.

"Is he okay?"

Kimo didn't know the answer to that. Had the fish been out of water too long? Had Kimo, in trying to save him, squeezed him to death?

"Find some water," he said.

Luckily they had a jug of drinking water with them. Kimo slid Goldie into it, and a second later, the fish began to swim as if nothing was wrong. Pippa, who rarely gave compliments, turned to Kimo. "That was amazing."

"Thanks," he said, but he was looking at Kim. "You too."

She nodded and smiled but didn't say anything. She was still in shock. Then the three oldest climbed out of the car to see the damage while Toby sat, clutching Goldie's jug hard against his heart.

What? What? What? Kim was chanting in her head as she kicked the car's burst tire. What? What?

What were they going to do? She didn't know.

Kimo stood watching her helplessly, but Pippa went around to the driver's side and pushed the button that popped the trunk. "What are you doing?" asked Kimo.

Pippa was bent over and rummaging around. A

second later, she pulled out a jackknife and flipped it open.

"You can't fix a tire with a knife," said Kimo, but Pippa had wandered away from the car and into the sugarcane field.

Pippa put the knife blade to a stalk of sugarcane and began to saw. As she worked the knife back and forth, she thought with some satisfaction that she was the one handling this crisis with the most aplomb; the other three had lost their cool. Maybe I'll be something dangerous when I grow up, she thought. A firefighter or a paramedic or a skydiver.

"Good idea," said Kimo as Pippa handed him a stalk of sugarcane. Even Kim stopped kicking long enough to take one. Still clutching Goldie, Toby emerged from the car and Pippa gave him one too. They stood sucking the sweetness from the sugarcane until Kim broke the silence, saying, "We need a house."

"We just need a tire," said Pippa. "If we can find a tire, we can put it on."

"How?" asked Kimo.

"We have a manual," said Pippa.

"We do?"

"In the glove compartment. At the bottom. I read it the day I found my glasses along with that book of yours."

"*The Perfects*," said Kim, her voice thick with admiration.

"No, not them, they're so boring. The book on the other side," said Pippa.

"*The Awfuls*," Kim said flatly.

"Yeah. Great story. I love that kid Leroy who leads them into the woods."

Kim wanted to defend *The Perfects*. She wanted to tell Pippa that she could learn a thing or two about good behavior from those Perfect children. Now that she thought about it, she would also have liked to say to Pippa that *The Awfuls* was a ridiculous book. It was so ridiculous that if Kim ever met the author (who had once lived on their island), she planned to tell her that the end of *The Awfuls* didn't make any sense at all. Children—especially misbehaved ones—didn't happen to find secret roads that led to magical cottages. But there was no time to say all this to Pippa, who couldn't be counted on not to lose her temper. So instead Kim said to her, "Grab that manual, would you?" Then she turned to Kimo. "Can we afford a new tire?"

"We only have nineteen dollars," said Kimo. They all knew a tire would cost more than that.

"Tina will drop off some money soon," Pippa offered as she fished in the glove compartment for the manual.

"What do we do till then? We can't sleep on the side of the road," Kim said.

"The playground," said Toby, who was nibbling on his sugarcane like it was an ear of corn.

"What are you talking about?" scolded Pippa. "We don't have time to go to the playground."

Toby shrugged and settled into silence. After a few minutes, Kim started smacking at the busted tire with her stew-can shoes. Toby could see how frustrated she was. "The playground at the beach," he tried again.

"What about it?" Kim snapped. She really did get annoyed at Toby sometimes.

"There's a tire."

Kim frowned at him. But Kimo said, "He's thinking of that tire hanging from the tree."

"That lousy tire swing?" Kim asked.

Toby nodded.

"A tire needs a rim," Kim said. "Tire swings don't have rims."

"The one at the beach does," said Pippa. "That's why it makes such a bad swing."

Kimo smiled at Toby. "You're a genius."

What the Fitzgerald-Trouts did next wasn't exactly legal, but I believe that it was necessary given the difficult situation they found themselves

in. After all,
they needed
a tire almost as
much as they
needed a house.
So that night
they walked to the
playground and untied the
rope that held the tire swing in
place. They felt guilty as they were doing it, but
when they inspected the tire and saw that it was
almost brand-new, the guilt went away, replaced
with glee. Once they'd taken it down, they hung
their old busted tire (which they had brought with
them) in its place, retying the rope. Pippa climbed
onto it and Kimo pushed her and she announced
that the soft, punctured tire without a rim was a
better swing anyway.

Afterward, on the beach, Toby held the flashlight while the oldest three studied the section of

the car's manual that described putting on a tire. "No problem," said Kimo when he'd finished reading.

"Easy peasy," Pippa agreed. They high-fived.

Kim didn't disagree, but as the others settled into the sand to sleep, she took the manual and began to study it. Paging through the descriptions of all those complicated car parts, she began to see how many different things could go wrong with their little green car: engine, brakes, exhaust, oil pan, steering wheel, gears. All those hardworking parts would be impossibly expensive to replace. The thought began to nudge at Kim and she couldn't get rid of it. All night she lay in the sand, squirming uncomfortably and looking up at the sky, which provided no shelter. At least when they slept in the car they had some kind of roof over their heads. Now they had nothing.

The next morning, when the sun was up and they'd had a swim, they began the long walk back to the car. They took turns rolling the new tire along beside them and when the tree-lined streets near the playground gave way to the sugarcane fields, Pippa used the jackknife to saw off more cane for a juicy breakfast.

Everyone was feeling relieved except Kim, who was still thinking about all those pages in the manual naming all those different car parts. Something else was sure to break sometime soon and then there would be many nights without a roof. Kim made a vow that as soon as the tire rolling beside her was on the car, she would do that thing that had been first on her to-do list for so long now. *Find a house.* She must find a house. But how?

How? How? How? She had no parents to help her; that was a given. Where else could she turn? What about the books she loved? With sudden rage, she thought how useless they all were. Most useless of all was *The Perfects*, which she had read so diligently. It had not given her a perfect life; instead, things were perfectly awful.

And that was when she thought of a book she

didn't love. She thought of *The Awfuls*. This was the kind of situation the Awfuls might face. What would those children do? Maybe it's time, Kim thought, to turn my book over and find a new kind of story.

CHAPTER
11

*B*umpity, *bumpity, bumpity, bump*—Kim raced the car down the island's worst road. *Bumpity, bumpity, bump.* You would think she would drive more slowly, having popped a tire the day before, but no, Kim was driving faster than ever. She had a plan for finding a house. A plan so crazy she didn't want anything to slow her down.

"What did you say we're doing?" asked Toby, who was holding Goldie in the jug.

"I didn't," said Kim.

As they raced along the last blocks of downtown and turned onto the coastal road, the potholes got worse. Kim kept apologizing for how fast she was going, but Kimo said he thought it actually made the bumps less noticeable.

Could it be that hitting a bump so fast flew them farther into the air and made them land less often and meant they hit fewer bumps? This seemed a good explanation to Kimo, but when he shared it with the others they looked at him blankly. They were caught up in their own concerns. Pippa was trying to keep her glasses on so that she could shout out the fonts on the signs that were getting less and less frequent the farther they got from downtown. Toby was trying to keep Goldie upright in his jug. Kim was trying to avoid potholes.

Beside them ran a long stretch of white-sand beach and beyond that, spilling to the horizon, the ocean, where waves swelled and grew and tumbled toward the shore. Toby thought about all the fish in that ocean, safe below the cresting waves, unlike poor Goldie, who was surfing in his jug.

Kimo was staring at the water, longing for a swim. He had done most of the work rolling the tire back to the car, and then replacing the busted tire with the new one. At one point, when the car had slipped off the tire jack that was holding it up, he'd grabbed the car and lifted it with his bare hands while Pippa bolted the new tire into place. Now he wanted nothing more than to jump into the water and wash all the dirt off himself. He was about to say so when suddenly the road veered farther inland, away from the shore, and Toby, who had been getting more and more upset watching Goldie, looked at Kim and said, "You don't have to tell us what we're doing, but maybe you could tell us where we're going."

It was the longest sentence to come out of Toby's mouth in ages—maybe ever—so Kim took it seriously.

"We're going…" she said. Then her voice trailed off. She knew what she was about to tell them would cause chaos, but she also knew she was going to have to admit it sooner or later. They weren't fools, her brothers and sister, and they would see soon enough where the road led. She decided to get it over with, and said very quickly, "The Sakahatchi."

She waited for the news to hit them like a wave.

"You're kidding, right?" said Kimo. "Do you know what happened to Ryan Lizzo when he tried to go in there? Did you see his scar?"

They had all seen the scar. Ryan Lizzo had paraded around school showing it to everyone. A scar as round and thick and raw-looking as a raspberry Danish. A gruesome scar that made every kid in that school jealous—though no one wanted to go through what Ryan Lizzo had gone through to get it.

Ryan Lizzo's father had taken Ryan Lizzo for a hike in the Sakahatchi Forest because Ryan Lizzo's father thought all the stories about the forest being filled with bloodsucking iguanas were old wives' tales.

But Ryan said that his father was wrong. And Ryan said that he had the scar to prove it.

"Ryan said they don't even have a name for those iguanas, the kind that bit him? They're so dangerous no one has even been able to identify them," said Kimo.

"Ryan told me they move so fast you don't see them coming," Pippa added. "They fly at you and they sink their teeth in your leg or your arm or your neck or whatever and then they hang on and they won't let go and all the time they're sucking your blood down their scaly throats."

Toby was the one who most liked forests, but even he said, "You can't make us go in there." Glancing in the rearview mirror, Kim saw that he had taken one hand off the goldfish's jug and was chewing his fingernails.

"Trust me," said Kim.

"I don't trust you," Pippa replied.

"You haven't had enough sleep," said Kimo. "You're not thinking right."

"It's going to be fine," said Kim. "If you don't trust me, at least trust my father. He always said he thought it was safe to go in the Sakahatchi at sunset. He said the forest is darker then, and so it's colder, and if there were iguanas they would move slower because of the cold."

"Oh, great," said Pippa. "We'll see the iguanas coming and we can try to get out of the way before they sink their teeth into us?"

"Something like that," said Kim, who realized how bonkers it sounded.

"Did our father ever try it?" asked Pippa. Kim wasn't about to admit that she didn't know.

"You can't trust your father," said Kimo. "Ryan Lizzo trusted his father—"

The rest was cut off by Pippa shouting *Look!* and pointing to a bright green sign with an arrow indicating a narrow dirt road that headed down toward the coast, disappearing into a thick stand of trees. The sign said: SAKAHATCHI FOREST. And then below was written: PROCEED AT YOUR OWN RISK.

Pippa said, "All caps. That's not a good sign."

"She's not talking about the font," said Kimo. "She's saying it's a bad *sign*! Like a bad omen!" Kimo turned sideways in his seat to talk directly to Kim, trying to convey to her what an awful idea this was. He wanted her to feel that special bond that they shared. The invisible thread. But Kim wasn't even looking at him.

"Don't turn down that road," Kimo said, but Kim was switching on her indicator. "Don't do it!" There was a steely quality to his voice that she'd never heard before, but she ignored it and turned the wheel. In the backseat, Pippa was watching the oldest siblings argue and thinking how for once she didn't have to try to stop bossy Kim. Kimo grabbed the steering wheel from Kim, wresting it the other way, trying to turn her from the Sakahatchi Forest road.

"Let go!" Kim shouted.

"You haven't even told us why you're doing this."

"Let go," Kim said. "Just let go!"

After what had happened to the tire the day before, you would think they would have known that what they were doing was terribly dangerous! It might have been more dangerous than the bloodsucking iguanas of the Sakahatchi Forest. Kimo must have realized this because he let go. Then he said, "We're not getting out of this car until you tell us what's going on."

"Then we won't get out of the car," said Kim.

And that was the compromise they made. They would go wherever Kim wanted, but they wouldn't get out of that car. Until that moment the windows had been down, but now they all reached for the window buttons. Pippa had her feet hanging outside, but she pulled them in as she rolled her window up.

Once they were on the dirt road leading down toward the Sakahatchi Forest, Kim found herself lifting her stew-can shoes ever so slightly off the gas pedal and slowing down. She realized now that her mad scheme (as she had called it back there walking on the road, rolling the tire) wasn't just a mad scheme, it was a mad, mad, mad scheme. A scheme that had gained in madness as she'd gotten closer to her goal.

Later Kim told me that if she were really going to be mathematical about it, she would probably say it wasn't just a mad scheme times three, but something more exponential, something like a mad scheme raised to the third power. The mad in the mad scheme was multiplied by itself three times!

The Scheme *wasn't*: Mad Scheme × 3

It *was*: (Mad × Mad × Mad) Scheme = $Mad^3$ Scheme

It was so mad she had decided never to admit it

to anyone, especially not to Pippa, because it was Pippa who had given her the spark of the idea for the scheme. Walking along by the side of the road, Kim had thought with rage about how none of the books she'd read could help her find a house. But then she'd thought of that book she almost never read: *The Awfuls*. The book that made her queasy. The book that Pippa had mentioned while they were eating sugarcane.

Unlike the Perfects, the Awful children didn't live in a beautiful house; they lived in a little shack owned by a mean landlord, who charged them rent and swatted their wrists with a wooden spoon when they couldn't pay. The only money the Awful children had came from cleaning the chimneys of the Perfect children's house. In the summertime, when the weather was hot and the Perfects stopped using their fireplace, the Awfuls had no work at all. Thus they had no money and no way to pay the mean landlord. Their wrists were very sore during those summer months, and they longed to escape.

Kim had only ever read *The Awfuls* once, but when they'd gotten the flat tire, Pippa had reminded her of the plot. She'd reminded Kim of how the oldest Awful boy, Leroy, had led his brothers and sisters on a journey to find a hiding place away from the mean landlord. After many awful adventures, Leroy and his siblings had found a secret road through some woods. The road led to the house of a long-lost uncle, who took them in. They never had to clean chimneys again or suffer another beating with that wooden spoon.

It was an ending that Kim had always found ridiculously unlikely and that was why her scheme was crazy. She was following the plot of a book she didn't like or believe. What was even crazier was that as she was coming up with her scheme, it had occurred to her that she and her brothers and sister must not journey into just any forest. They must go into a *dangerous* forest. She remembered Leroy telling the other Awfuls that only by risking something great would they find something great, like a house. And in the book Leroy had been right. So Kim drove on, following the advice of Leroy Awful. Hoping it wasn't awful advice.

As the little green car got closer to the stand of trees, the road narrowed and the warning signs (PROCEED AT YOUR OWN RISK) got more frequent. It didn't make any of them feel any less anxious that the sun was setting. The shadows of the trees were growing longer until at last the little car was consumed by darkness.

Kim turned on the headlights just in time to see that they were reaching the end of the dirt road. There was no way through the woods. No secret path. There was nothing in front of the car but enormous, tall trees with massive trunks, the kind of trees the ancient islanders used to cut down and carve into canoes.

As she had promised, Kim did not ask the others to get out of the car and walk. But she did keep going. She found that the space between the trees was big enough to drive through. She

pressed down on the gas pedal and steered the car up and over the tree roots. The little green car with its fearful crew moved deeper into the roadless woods.

Well, Kim thought, we never were like the Perfects. We always were more like the Awfuls. Kim was surprised to feel a strange swelling in her heart that seemed a little bit like pride.

This feeling of pride lasted about four seconds and ended with a *thwack* when a large, angry, hissing Sakahatchi iguana launched itself out of the darkness and onto the windshield. Before the children could even scream, *thwack*—another iguana hit the side window, and another, and another—*thwack, thwack, thwack*.

Now the *thwack*s were punctuated by the shouts of the three youngest Fitzgerald-Trouts, screaming at Kim to turn around. "I'm not turning around," said Kim, adding quite reasonably, "they aren't hurting us."

Somehow, to Kim, the iguana attack meant that the journey was suitably dangerous and if they kept on, if she kept on, they might fulfill their quest and find a place to live or possibly a kindhearted uncle.

Seeing that Kim was bent on continuing and not wanting to grab the wheel, which might cause them to hit a tree, the younger Fitzgerald-Trouts quieted down. They sat, chewing their fingernails, listening to the thumping on the car's roof and watching the fat green reptiles shoot out of the

darkness and smack against the glass, where they stuck for a second before sliding out of sight.

How many times had they driven that car to the drive-in to stare through the windshield at a horror movie with killer zombies or dinosaurs? Now it was as if one of those terrifying movies had come to life around them.

And it didn't stop. *Thwack, thwack, thwack*— the iguanas bombarded the car. Three or four iguanas now gripped the windshield wipers. Kim turned the wipers on, hoping to bat the iguanas away, but they just stayed there, prehistoric yellow eyes glaring at her through the glass, as the wipers bumped against their scaly bodies.

Pippa shuddered and took her glasses off, saying, "Our dad was wrong," then adding with a sigh, "of course he was."

They drove for an hour between the trees, up and over the roots. Kim was driving so slowly, pressing on the gas pedal so cautiously (despite her heavy stew-can shoes) that the muscles of her right leg had begun to throb. They hadn't gone very far into the woods, but Kim began to suspect that they'd gone farther than any other humans before them.

There were no signs anymore. There certainly wasn't any kind of road or trail. Even the iguanas seemed not to have penetrated this far into the woods because the thwacking noise had petered out and the last two iguanas, gripping the windshield wipers, had closed their eyes and fallen asleep. At some point, as the car drove through low-hanging branches, both iguanas were swept off the hood and vanished into the dark undergrowth.

"Maybe our father wasn't completely wrong." Kim spoke into the eerie silence of the car. Only Kimo was awake (he was holding Goldie now). The two youngest had fallen asleep in the backseat. "You just have to enter the forest when it's really late and really dark."

"Maybe," said Kimo grudgingly. To tell the horrible truth, during that long stretch while the youngest two slept, something had shifted in Kimo's feelings toward Kim. Not only was Kimo not feeling kindly toward her, but for the first time in his life he was feeling angry. If they really shared that invisible thread, wouldn't Kim have explained to him what they were doing out there in the forest? After Pippa and Toby had fallen asleep, Kim had had every chance to explain. But she hadn't. She had decided what to do all on her own. Like always. Kimo pulled his feet up onto the seat and wrapped his arms around his knees as if to signal that he was closing up shop. He wasn't going to take orders from Kim anymore.

What he didn't know was that Kim was so embarrassed by her mad scheme that she had clammed up. The farther they drove, the more clearly Kim saw that soon she would have to admit defeat and turn the car around. As if to add to her feelings of shame, Pippa's stomach and Toby's stomach began to grumble loudly. If Kim hadn't been steering over a particularly gnarled tree root, she would have hung her head. How could she have thought her scheme more important than feeding her little brother and little sister?

Kimo was wondering the same thing, and he was trying to think of something cutting to say

to her. Just as the words were taking shape on his lips, light suddenly flooded the car. The moon had broken through the trees and was shining down, bathing them in radiance.

They looked up and saw the stars blinking in the sky above. Kimo could see those same stars reflected in Goldie's jug. At that moment, they realized that the forest was coming to an end. Kim rolled down the window and took a deep breath. "Ocean," she said. She could smell the salt carried on the breeze. She could hear the waves—a cease-less roar, like the sound of an enormous washing machine. "We're getting close to the coast."

"Forget about the coast," Kimo said. "Look at that." The car had emerged from the trees into a wide, open space. If the space had been filled with water, you would have said it was some kind of large and mysterious whirlpool because the top of it seemed to be swirling and moving in low, rip-pling waves. But the space wasn't filled with water, and as Kim drove the car down into it and the headlights illuminated a multitude of thin green shafts, Kimo realized it was a meadow filled with tall grass.

The swirling surface was the tips of the grass rippling as it moved with the wind coming off the ocean. Kimo had never seen anything like it.

Even more strange, as the car parted the grass, they could see, far up ahead of them, a dark shape looming. A shape like the little matchbox Pippa carried in her pocket, if that matchbox had worn a triangular hat. Even as she was thinking this, Kim realized the shape wasn't little at all. It only looked little because it was so very far away.

What large object made a shape like a rectangle with a triangle on top? The only thing Kim could think of was a house. The rectangle must be a house and the triangle must be its roof. Was the shape on the distant horizon the fulfillment of their dreams?

By the time they reached the shape, Kimo was shaking Toby and Pippa awake. Pippa had been dreaming about a talking tiger who would tell her

his secrets if she fed him cheese. Toby was having the dream he always had about a black monkey climbing up the side of a house. Being woken suddenly, not knowing where they were—it seemed to Pippa and Toby that they were leaving one dream and entering another.

When they saw the house, they were absolutely sure it was a dream. Toby thought he was finally going to catch that black monkey.

Kim threw the car into park and leapt out, leaving the headlights on so that they could see. Kimo grabbed a flashlight anyway. Without saying a word, the four children took one another's hands and waded through the tall grass toward the front door. Kim was still wearing her stew-can shoes, but she didn't care.

*Bang! Bang! Bang!* Kimo knocked loudly. They stood poised on the front stoop, hearts beating fast, waiting for whatever came next.

Only nothing happened. There was no answer. Pippa grabbed ahold of the doorknob and tried to turn it, but the door was locked tight. "Shoot!" she said, and sighed, feeling very hungry. She had been hoping to enter the house and find a kitchen filled with cheese and maybe a talking tiger.

"Let me try." Kimo shoved Kim and Pippa out of the way. He put the flashlight between his teeth and took hold of the knob, shaking it fiercely. But the door didn't budge.

"Maybe there's another way in," suggested Kim, and so they began to walk around the house, spreading out to cover more ground. Each of them wanted to be the one who discovered another door or an open window—or some way to penetrate the wooden boards of that strange place.

Toby and Pippa were just rounding the far side and had spotted a back door when they heard a bloodcurdling scream from the front. It sounded like Kim.

"The iguanas!" shouted Pippa as she scrambled through the dark grass back toward the front door. But when Pippa arrived, Kim didn't have bloodsucking iguanas hanging from her; instead she was standing in front of a tall, long-haired woman who was looking at her out of the darkness with terrifying, unblinking eyes. Even though Kim was wearing those tall stew-can shoes, the woman towered above her. Pippa waited for the woman to shout at Kim or at least say something, but she just kept staring.

A second later, Kimo arrived with the flashlight. Kim was pointing at the woman and managed to choke out, "What is it?"

Kimo lifted his flashlight and ran its beam up and down the woman's body. She was not human at all. She was the wooden figurehead from an old sailing ship. She had been hung up on a high peg nailed into the front of the house as if she were still on the prow of a boat.

Kimo directed the flashlight at her face and got up on his tiptoes to get a better look. There was something familiar about her. Something he could barely untangle from his memory. And then, in a flash, a memory came to him: Someone was holding him and lifting him toward the woman's face, and that someone was saying the word *siren*. He thought the person might have been his father.

"I've seen her before," Kimo said. "In the harbor. On a boat. When I was little."

"Wow," said Pippa. "How did she end up here?"

"Have you ever heard the word *siren*?" Kimo asked. "I mean, besides like a siren on a police car or something."

"I think it means mermaid."

And sure enough, when Kimo traced his flashlight over the figure, they saw that out of her long torso and her very long curls of hair there emerged a fish's tail.

"Whatever she is," said Kim, "she's not going to hurt us."

Just then a window slid open. "Hey," said Toby. He was calling to them from inside. The whole time they'd been standing looking at the siren, Toby had been making his way into the house through a tiny swinging door cut into the back. When he opened the back door for the others, he showed it to them. "That's a dog door," Kim explained.

"Maybe it's for a tiger," said Pippa.

Once inside, they flipped on the lights and rushed to the kitchen. They were so hungry! Though the fridge was empty, the kitchen shelves were lined with hundreds and hundreds of cans of food.

Kimo found a can opener and set to work. Each of them held their own fork, taking a few bites before passing a can along. They ate tuna fish, water chestnuts, mandarin oranges, and baked beans. SPAM, peas, peaches, and creamed corn. Prunes, pumpkin, kimchee, and green beans. Jack-fruit, chickpeas, Vienna sausages, and corned beef hash. The oldest three tried the curried prawns, but Toby did not. Instead he ate a whole can of lychees in syrup. And between them they consumed twelve servings of rice pudding.

They ate things in no particular order and they ate things cold; they were so hungry they didn't want to waste time heating anything up. They ate and ate and ate. Eating made them realize how hungry they really were. They ate faster and faster. It was a feast unlike any they had ever had.

Eventually their eating slowed. They stopped opening cans because they were having trouble eating the ones that were still open. Soon they didn't want another bite. But they didn't want to waste the food either. It was a situation they had never faced before. Anyone else might have put the food in the fridge, but the Fitzgerald-Trouts weren't used to living with a fridge. So they soldiered on, eating until the last open can was scraped clean.

It was well past midnight when the siblings tossed all those empty cans into the sink and stumbled out of the kitchen. Their stomachs were full and now they were going to find places to curl up. Kim's mad scheme had paid off. That night the Fitzgerald-Trout children would sleep in a house.

The next morning, as Kimo drifted out of sleep, the thought came to him that he had spent the night in a house. His eyes blinked open, the better to see if this was true. He discovered that it was. Overhead was a high, wooden-beamed roof. Below him he could feel the soft cushions of a couch. Strangest of all, his legs did not hurt because he had not slept upright. He closed his eyes again and lay there soaking in the feeling of being flat. Of course he'd slept flat on the beach before, but a beach wasn't as soft as a couch and he'd always woken with sand in his ears and nose and mouth.

Kimo's mind began to trace the events that had led them to the house. With this came the memory that he had been really angry at Kim. He felt that memory stir and he tested it out. Was he still angry? He realized, happily, that he wasn't angry at all. So Kim hadn't told him what they were doing. That was just how she was. Kim was Kim. She was never going to change. Being angry at her would be like being angry at the ocean if you got tossed by a wave.

Kim, lying in a little bed on the other side of the wall, had no idea Kimo had just forgiven her. She lay tucked away in a small bedroom where there was nothing much but a trundle bed and an old wooden desk with a typewriter on it, and she was experiencing a rare moment of solitude.

She looked up. In the clear light of morning she could see that there were cobwebs hanging from the light fixture. She looked over at the wall where a narrow set of bookshelves hung. The night before, she had studied the books. Their titles—*Halfway Across the Pacific*, *The Voyage of the* Beagle, *Journey of the Whaling Ship* Essex—suggested that the owner of the house was fond of adventures. Now she saw with delight that all the books were coated with dust and that cobwebs joined them, spine to spine. The typewriter was dusty too and littered with the bodies of dead flies.

The more closely Kim looked, the more clearly she saw that there were dead flies scattered over everything, like the confetti you throw when you are celebrating. And Kim was celebrating! Because she was pretty sure those cobwebs and flies meant that no one had been in the house for a while, and that meant no one was likely to return anytime soon. Maybe she really had crossed out that first item on her to-do list. *Find a house.*

To be clear, the place wasn't what most people would call a house, though Kim and the others thought of it that way. It was what I call a cabin. It was a simple, one-story wooden building on the edge of a cliff overlooking the ocean. It had two small bedrooms, a tiny kitchen, an even smaller bathroom, and a very large, open front room with windows that gave a view of the sea. The furniture was minimal; the bedding (discovered the night before in the cabin's only closet) was moth-eaten; the wooden floors were uncarpeted and the wooden walls unpainted. It was a very simple place, one whose only luxury appeared to be that it had electricity because, like so many houses on that island, there were solar panels on the roof.

Kim was running her hand happily through a pile of dust when she noticed that there was a piece of paper sticking out of the type-writer. She got up out of bed to take a look and found that someone had typed a few sentences onto it.

Kim pulled the paper

out of the typewriter and began to read: "My sister and I were born two minutes apart. She was born just one minute before midnight and I was born just one minute after. Because of this, though we are twins, we always celebrated our birthday on different days. We had different parties and different cakes. But because we had the same friends we invited the same guests...."

That was all the paper said. How mysterious, Kim thought, and she began to look through the desk for other pieces of paper—some note or scribbling that might explain the sentences or at least give them a context. But the drawers were all empty.

Just as Kim was beginning to read the mysterious sentences again, Toby came into the room, carrying Goldie and looking guilty. "We left him in the car last night."

"How did he sleep?" Kim asked, deciding to forget about the piece of paper and be nice to Toby for once.

"He was on the dashboard." Toby's lip quivered.

"He likes the dashboard," Kim said, taking Goldie's jug from Toby. "How about we put him there?" She pointed to the bookshelves.

"He wants a view," Toby said.

So they left the little room and settled Goldie onto the mantel over the fireplace in the living room, where Kimo was still stretched out on the couch and Pippa was playing with a pair of binoculars she had found. "That's a good place for Goldie," Pippa said as Toby adjusted Goldie's bowl on the mantel. "He can watch the lava gulls from there." She gestured out the window to the birds swooping in the air above the ocean and diving down to catch their morning breakfast.

"Goldie's part of the reason I drove through the woods and found this place," Kim offered. "If it hadn't been for Goldie, we might have stayed in that car a lot longer."

Toby shrugged and said, "I guess."

"Doesn't it make you happy to see him here, looking at the ocean? And watching the lava gulls will make him glad he's in a jug where he can't be eaten."

"Maybe," said Toby, who was feeling a little like a goldfish trapped in a jug. He was missing the car and the beach and the forest and wondering why everyone seemed so happy about the house.

"You okay?" asked Kim.

"Hungry," said Toby.

"Me too," said Pippa. The night before it hadn't seemed possible that any of them would ever be hungry again. But there it was, that gnawing in all their stomachs. Together the Fitzgerald-Trouts headed for the kitchen.

That morning was a Sunday and the children didn't have to go to school. Which was lucky because the sun was already shining and the forest was warming up and the iguanas were most certainly rousing themselves. Eventually they were going to have to face those iguanas, but they wanted to put it off as long as possible.

Over breakfast, Kim told them her theory that

all the dust and the dead flies meant the owner had been away for a long time. "I don't think he'll be back for a while," she said.

"But if he's been away a long time, he might be back much sooner," said Kimo. "Nobody leaves a house forever."

"Why do you keep saying 'he'?" asked Pippa. "He might be a she."

"He or she might have a twin," Kim said. They looked at her in surprise. "I found some writing on a piece of paper in the typewriter...." She lapsed for a second into a broody silence. She was thinking that Kimo was probably right; no one stays away from a house forever.

"Well," said Kimo, sensing her mood, "we're here for right now. Let's enjoy it." They all nodded in agreement, even Kim.

After breakfast they each wandered off to do their own thing. Kim played in the kitchen trying out all the gadgets. She knew a little bit about appliances because, like all sixth graders, she had

helped in the school kitchen, so she found a couple of loaves of day-old bread in the trunk of the car and made toast for all of them. Then she looked for things to put on top of it. Toast with canned meat? Toast with vegetables? Toast slathered with mushimush-berry jam? She would have tried the oven, but she had no flour, no milk, no eggs. None of the things that you need to bake. Instead she made more and more toast.

While Kim was in the kitchen, Toby, Kimo, and Pippa were exploring the outdoors. The first thing they did was to go look at the siren. In the broad light of day, she didn't look the least bit terrifying. In fact, though her wood was cracked and the bright paint that had once distinguished her face was faded, she was somehow beautiful. Kimo was certain he had seen her before.

At the back of the house, Pippa found a flagpole with a flag flying from it. The flag looked brand-new and was white with the profile of a dog's head stamped on it. If the house were a ship, the flag would have been flying from its stern. Kimo thought it was very strange that the flag looked so new. It wasn't tattered or faded. It made him worry that the owner had been there recently.

Kim had been trying out the kitchen's blender and came outside with a jug of a fruity drink she'd made. She offered an empty cup to each of them and filled it with a bright red liquid. They sipped. Delicious! The shadow of a lava gull passed over them and they watched it as it drifted out over the meadow. "I think they keep the iguanas away," said Pippa, who had been watching the birds. "I'm going to find out." She headed back to the house to get the binoculars.

She settled onto the edge of the cliff, where the noise of the birds was deafening. Through the binoculars, she saw that there were thousands and thousands of nests in the cliff face and that each had at least one baby. She watched a grown-up lava gull leave its nest and soar out from the cliff, searching for food. It made slow, lazy movements above the ocean until it saw the silver ripple of a fish, then—*whoosh*—it plummeted fifty feet down to the water, scooped the fish up in its beak, and delivered the fish back to its hungry fledgling.

As Pippa watched, she saw that there was nothing terrible about lava gull parents. The more the babies cried, the harder their parents worked to make them happy. Those parents were devoted to their insatiable, demanding offspring. How different this was from Pippa's own experience. When I'm a mom, thought Pippa, I'm going to be like that. Then she thought guiltily of her doll, Lani. Pippa had had Lani for as long as she could remember, but it had been a while since she'd played with her. She left the cliff and walked back to the car, fishing in the trunk until she found Lani, facedown and under the toolbox. "I'm sorry," she said to the doll, kissing her on the forehead and straightening her dress.

Meanwhile Kimo and Toby were walking

farther into the deep grass of the meadow, which, they were discovering, was full of treasures. They found an old campfire and the brittle remains of a tent. They found an antique bathtub. They found a crusty but still workable scuba suit hanging on the branches of a tree. Toby found a bunch of old paint canisters and plastic buckets, which he quickly turned upside down and began to play like they were drums.

Most wonderful of all, around lunchtime, they discovered the remains of an old airplane. At least they thought it was an airplane—it had two engines, a propeller, and a set of panels that seemed to have once belonged to a round fuselage. But no matter how hard they looked they couldn't find any wings. Could there be an airplane without wings?

Kimo went back to the house and rummaged around until he found a machete in the broom closet. He used that machete to cut through the tall meadow grass around the plane. He was looking for the plane's wings, but he found only nuts and bolts and other small mechanical parts.

They ate lunch with their feet hanging over the cliff. Kim had been busy in the kitchen, and there was more toast—this time with peanut butter—and more tropical drinks. As they ate, they talked about the mystery of the wingless plane. Kimo was his practical self. "The wings have to be somewhere," he said. "They didn't just vanish."

"I think they did," said Toby, who loved a mystery.

"Maybe someone threw them over the cliff." Kimo shrugged.

"That's littering," piped up Pippa. She had Lani in her lap and was feeding the doll bites of sandwich. "Who would do that?"

Kim began to imagine, "What if you loved someone and they were going to fly away and you didn't want them to? Maybe you would take the wings from their plane and throw them in the water."

"You've been reading too many books," said Pippa.

"Maybe the wings were made of something that melts." That was Kimo.

"Like what?" asked Toby.

"I dunno," said Kimo, wrinkling his forehead in thought. "Like maybe salt or sugar...or wax."

"That's just dumb." Pippa didn't mince words. "The wings wouldn't be strong enough to fly if they were made out of something that melts. What if it got hot? They'd melt while you were flying."

"Hey," said Kimo, "maybe that's why the plane crashed. The wings melted."

"Did it crash?" Toby asked. That was news to him.

"Who knows?" said Kim.

"I bet there never were wings," Pippa mused.

"Are there planes that can fly without wings?" And so the conversation went. Round and round. Until the toast was gone and the cups were empty. Toby was so excited by the mystery of the missing wings that he forgot how much he was missing the forest. Kim and Kimo forgot to worry about the house's owner coming back.

After lunch, to avoid letting the worrying thought back into their heads, Kimo suggested a swim. They spread out along the cliff face looking for a way down to the water. After a little while, Pippa, who had walked the farthest, shouted to the others, "Over here."

She had found a small path lined with spice bushes. It looked very steep and they couldn't quite tell if it went all the way to the beach, but Kimo decided to try it. He held on to a bush and slid partway down, then he grabbed another bush and slid farther. He went on like that until they couldn't see him anymore. A few minutes later he shouted up at them, "Beach!"

By the time they were all standing on the sand, the sun was sliding down the sky. Like many of us islanders, the children thought this was the perfect time of day for a swim. Without thinking twice, they jumped into the ocean in their clothes, swimming as far out beyond the reef as they dared. Far from the cliff, floating on the open water, with the ocean floor hundreds of feet below them, they splashed around. They dove down and did somersaults, then rose out of the water and spit in one another's faces. When a wave came, they slid up and over it. Kimo sank deep into the water and let himself think about his father. Had it been Johnny Trout who had held him up and showed him the face of the siren?

As the sun sank beyond the horizon, they watched for the green flash that comes just as the light disappears. When they saw it, they shouted "Zap!" and poked one another.

Later, while darkness seeped into the sky like squid ink, they floated on their backs and watched the stars come out. One of the best things about not having parents was that there was no one to tell them not to swim in their clothes, no one to tell them it was dangerous to swim after dark, and

no one to tell them it was time to go in. They went back to shore when they wanted, catching a wave up onto the narrow band of sand that sat at the foot of the cliff. They climbed up the steep cliff face, holding on to the spice bushes so that they didn't slide backward. When they were all assembled at the top, they headed together into the house to make dinner.

Once in the house, the mood of elation began to slip away. The day had slid into darkness and so had the children's thoughts. Kim was thinking how the owner could be on the way home right now, but Pippa, Kimo, and Toby were thinking something even worse. They were thinking that the next morning they would have to go back to school and that would mean once again driving through the forest and facing the bloodsucking iguanas.

As Pippa twisted the handle of the can opener, her mind turned over the problem. What would keep those iguanas away? If only iguanas could read, she would make a sign that said KEEP OFF THE CAR and she would hang it from the car's hood. I'll make the letters big, she thought. What font should I use? And then she thought of Mr. Knuckles's laundromat sign with those tiny spikes to keep the pigeons off. What if I use Pigeon font to stop them?

It didn't take much explaining for the others to get on board. After dinner, they found everything they needed in the little shed attached to the back of the house, and they went to work building Pigeon font—or in this case, Iguana font. In the end they had enough stuff to make six contraptions. The contraptions were long pieces of wood with nails hammered through them so that they poked out the other side. Squeezing a healthy dose of superglue onto each of them, the children fastened those rows of spikes along the hood and roof of the car. Then they stood back to admire their work.

It might not stop the iguanas entirely but it would definitely scare them off.

The next morning, when the children headed into the forest with their windows rolled up and the windshield wipers going, three iguanas launched themselves at the car. *Thwack, thwack, thwack.* But the rows of spikes were waiting. As soon as the iguanas landed on them, their jaws snapped open, their yellow eyes flashed, and they dove off the car.

"It's working," said Pippa, pressing Lani's face to the glass to show the doll the forest.

"Maybe they're smart," said Kimo. "Maybe when we drive back through tonight, they'll see the spikes and they won't attack us at all."

"I never thought I'd want a bloodsucking iguana to be smart," said Kim. She was following the tracks that the car had taken when they'd arrived—between the trees, up and over the roots. "If we keep driving back and forth, this is gonna turn into a road."

"Let's keep driving back and forth," said Kimo, who had once again slept very well in the little house.

"Let's," agreed Pippa.

"As long as the owner doesn't come back," Kim replied. As if to punctuate her remark, a huge iguana hit the windshield with a *thwack* and stared at them for a moment before the wipers shoved him onto the spikes and he jumped in surprise from the car.

Not much has been said about Kimo and Toby's mother, Tina. It really hasn't seemed necessary because except for her visits to tell the children to wash their hands and do their homework, Tina was such a small part of their lives. But around the time that the Fitzgerald-Trouts discovered the house, something happened that changed all that. One of Tina's songs suddenly became the number one hit on the island's pop-music charts. The song was called "Your Lyin' Heart," and it was very catchy. Tina sang it with a country-and-western twang that Pippa could mimic perfectly.

> *Your lyin' heart*
> *Will tear us apart*
> *And then I start—*
> *A-cryin'*

Though they knew every word of the song, none of them quite understood the lyrics. Toby, for instance, thought it was "Your Lion Heart" and that the song was about a lion who tore his friend apart. Kim had to explain that the song was about someone who lied to someone who loved him.

"I don't get it," said Pippa. "If he lies, why does she love him?"

"Why's she even sad? He's a jerk," said Toby.

"I hate liars," said Kimo.

"Get rid of him," Pippa declared.

"Do you think Tina's singing about the man with the blue suit?" asked Kimo.

"When he comes to bring us money we should ask him," said Pippa. They all snickered thinking about what he would say if they did.

"Have you ever noticed," said Kim, "how his bald head is bright red?"

"He needs to wear sunscreen," said Pippa.

"He needs to get a roof for his car," said Kimo.

A few days later, they were driving through the woods on their way to town, and crooning along in unison, "Your lyin' heart will tear us apart," when suddenly Pippa added, "And make me fart." They all burst out laughing.

"Wait, I got one," said Kim, snapping off the radio. "Your lyin' heart will tear us apart, and make me fart, or bake a lemon tart…"

"How 'bout this," shouted Pippa. "Your lyin' heart will tear us apart, and make me fart, or bake a lemon tart, or…paint funny art?"

"Or go to Kmart," said Kimo.

"Or stab you with a dart." (That was Toby.)

"Or grow a wart."

"Or tame a wild shark."

All day long, any time there was a lull in the conversation, someone would shout out a new lyric.

"Or learn a martial art!"

"Or draw a pie chart."

"Or eat à la carte."

"Or throw the car in park." (That was Kim.)

So on that afternoon when they pulled into the laundromat parking lot to do a load of laundry and buy some day-old bread, Toby happened to be shouting, "Or buy a Toastie Tart."

"That's a good idea," said Kim, who was unlacing her stew-can shoes. "We can try them in the toaster tonight." Kim pulled her notebook out of her pocket and glanced quickly at her to-do list and then at the one she'd made for Kimo. "You start the laundry," she said to him, not seeing that he was already collecting the dirty clothes that were strewn around the car.

Toby went with Kim to buy the Toastie Tarts, and Pippa (and Lani) went with Kimo to do the laundry.

Mr. Knuckles greeted them as the bell chimed and they walked through the door. "Vending machine no broke," he said, giving Kimo a sad face.

"It's okay," said Kimo. "Kim's buying Toastie Tarts."

Kimo loaded the laundry into the washer, tossed in some detergent, and plugged the slot with four quarters. Immediately a loud rush of water poured into the machine, and Kimo and Pippa headed for the plastic seats, where they could read magazines and watch the clothes go around and around.

"How you kids?" Mr. Knuckles asked.

"Okay," said Kimo.

"Mother get thirty-five years," said Mr. Knuckles, gesturing toward a newspaper next to the cash register.

"Mother, like, our mother?" Pippa asked. Mr. Knuckles nodded and showed them the photo of Maya Fitzgerald on the cover.

"At least this time she isn't wearing pajamas," said Pippa. After Pippa had skimmed the article and sighed at the fate of her mother, she set down the paper, and her eye caught sight of something hanging over the cash register. "Hey, Kimo," she said, "doesn't that look like our flag?"

Kimo turned and looked at where she was pointing. There was a picture hanging above the cash register that looked like the same profile of the dog's head.

"What's that, Mr. Knuckles?" Pippa asked.

"Map," Mr. Knuckles said, and shrugged. "Wabo Point."

"It's a map?" asked Kimo, getting up out of his chair and crossing to the picture. Sure enough, if you were close to it you could see that the dog's profile was formed by the shape of the coast outlined on a map. "A map of what?"

"Wabo Point," Mr. Knuckles said again.

"Where's that?"

"Past Sakahatchi Forest. No go. Iguanas. But Wabo is good. Fishing nice. You go on boat. Not through forest."

"Are you saying," asked Kimo, "that the place

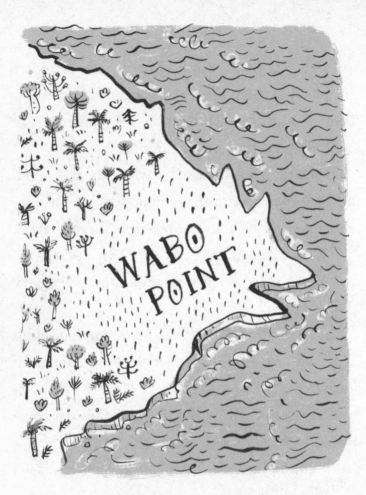

beyond the Sakahatchi Forest is called Wabo Point and it's shaped like the head of a dog?"

"Yeah," said Mr. Knuckles. "Wabo mean dog."

That was when Pippa and Kimo both

remembered learning in school that *wabo* was the word for dog in the native language of the island.

Kim and Toby had just pushed through the door, carrying their bags of groceries. "Check this out," said Kimo. "It's a map of our point. Wabo Point. It's shaped like a dog's head."

"The flag," said Kim, getting it at once.

"You kids never heard about Wabo?" asked Mr. Knuckles. They all shook their heads. "What they teach you in school anyhow?"

"Math," said Pippa, "and spelling and stuff."

"Wabo important," said Mr. Knuckles, tapping the spaceship tattoo on his arm. The children were confused. What was the connection between Wabo Point and a spaceship? Mr. Knuckles went on to explain that for many years the origins of the island's first settlers had been argued. Some historians thought that hundreds of years ago the settlers had come in canoes from a country in the east. Other historians thought that hundreds of years ago the settlers had come in canoes from a country in the west. The children already knew this much, and they were nodding and trying to get Mr. Knuckles to hurry the story along. Kimo even reminded Mr. Knuckles that his own father, Johnny Trout, had been lost at sea trying to prove the west-believers' side of the argument.

"What about the tattoo?" Kimo asked, and that was when Mr. Knuckles explained that there were a few people—like himself—who believed that the first settlers of the island came from some-where else entirely.

"Where?"

Mr. Knuckles cleared his throat and then he leaned across the counter and said, very seriously, "Outer space."

"What?" they all exclaimed at once.

"*Outer space!*" Mr. Knuckles yelled. "Outer space," he said more quietly.

"They were aliens?" asked Toby.

"Why else they call it Wabo Point?" said Mr. Knuckles. "How else they know it shape like dog's head except they come in spaceship from sky?"

"That's incredible," said Kimo.

Mr. Knuckles tapped a photograph in an ornate wooden frame that hung beside the map of Wabo Point. "This our club."

The children went around the counter to look at the picture that showed a group of men and women standing in two rows. The men were dressed in suits and ties and had unsmiling expressions on their faces. Engraved on the frame in gold (and in Helvetica font, Pippa told them later) were the letters IDOOS.

"What's IDOOS?" Kimo asked.

"Island Descendants of Outer Space," answered Mr. Knuckles. "I'm the treasurer. We took picture last meeting? You come next time, you like."

"Oh, no thank you," said Kim quickly. "It's got nothing to do with us." She was making eyes at all of them not to say too much. She didn't want them giving away the fact that they were living anywhere near Wabo Point.

"You island children, aren't you?" Mr. Knuckles stomped his foot. "You descended from the first settlers!"

"We're Fitzgerald-Trouts," said Kim, putting an end to the discussion.

Smiling at Mr. Knuckles and thanking him for the lesson, they backed away from the counter and went to sit on the plastic chairs in front of the laundry machines.

Pippa leaned forward and looked at them all gravely. "Do you think an alien owns our house?"

"I doubt it," said Kim.

"Nah," said Kimo.

"I hope so," said Toby.

The sun had set when the children came out of the laundromat and headed for the car. Exhausted and hungry, they swung open the car door and a howling sound poured out, making their hair stand up on end.

"What is it?" cried Kim, who couldn't see anything in the weak overhead light of the parking lot.

Kimo, Toby, and Pippa had their heads in the backseat and were staring at whatever was making the howling noise. They didn't answer. The car was going *ping, ping, ping* to say that the door was open, and the three of them were standing there staring down at the howling thing. Kim could see that the overhead car light was on, but she couldn't see what they were looking at, and for a second the thought crossed her mind that an alien had appeared in their backseat.

"What?" Kim shouted. "What is making that racket?" She shoved between them and plunged her head into the light. Strapped into a car seat that was carefully belted into the back was a little baby, its mouth open wide and bawling.

"A baby?" Kim couldn't believe it. "A baby?"

"A baby," the others echoed as Kim unstrapped the poor little thing and cradled it in her arms. She pulled it out of the car and rocked it. "Hush, hush, shhh," she cooed, but the baby kept on howling. "Give me something to make it stop," she said.

Toby opened one of the shopping bags, ripped open a box, and handed Kim a Toastie Tart. It was the best they could do. So Kim let the little baby suck on the corner of it, and the baby slowly quieted down.

"Where'd he come from?" asked Pippa.

"Aliens," said Toby.

"Don't be silly," said Kim, though she'd thought the same thing. She held the baby close to the back-seat light and peeked inside its diaper. "She's a she, by the way. Not a he."

"She is?"

"Why would someone leave us a baby?" asked Kimo.

"You really have to ask?" said Kim.

"Yes, I do," said Kimo. "Why us?"

"She looks just like Toby when he was little," said Kim. "Same little wrinkled chin, same green eyes, same turned-up nose."

And then the penny dropped for all of them, and they understood what Kim had understood from the moment she'd seen the baby. The baby was their sister. The newest, youngest Fitzgerald-Trout, born to Tina, the terrible mother. Tina had left her there in the backseat of the car for them to find.

"She couldn't even face us herself," said Pippa. "She just left it and ran."

"She hasn't dropped by in months," said Kimo. "She's been sending her boyfriend."

"She was pregnant. She didn't want us to know," said Kim, rocking the baby back and forth just as she had done with Toby when he was little. "And don't call her an *it*."

"You think her father is the man in the blue convertible?" asked Kimo.

"Probably," said Kim.

Pippa, who cared about these things and liked to know exactly how to draw the family tree, piped up. "Do we have to count him as one of our fathers? Five parents is really confusing and we don't even know his first name."

"You can count him if you want," said Kim. "But you don't have to."

"What if some of us count him and some of us don't?" asked Pippa.

"We'll figure it out later," said Kimo.

"Speaking of names," said Kim, "what should we name her?"

And they all looked at the baby in Kim's arms. The baby smiled up at them. "Penny," Toby said.

"Penny?"

"Find a penny, pick it up, all day long you'll have good luck," he said, repeating what they all said every time they found a coin lying on the ground.

"We did find her," said Kim. "And we picked her up, and we could use some good luck to keep the owner of the house away."

"We're gonna need more than luck for that," said Pippa. She was wishing she'd come up with the name.

"She's already good luck," said Kimo, who had just emerged from the backseat, where he'd been fishing around to see what else the terrible mother had left. "Look." He held up the envelope Tina had shoved into a bag of diapers. In the envelope was a wad of money, and Kimo was counting it. When he finished he said, "Eighty dollars. More than the usual."

" 'Your Lyin' Heart' really is paying off," said Pippa.

"I hope she and the man in the blue convertible are very, very happy," said Kim. They could tell from the sound of Kim's voice that she didn't mean it at all.

Kim handed Penny to Kimo, who tucked her into her car seat while Pippa and Toby climbed in, each of them taking hold of one of Penny's tiny little hands. "Let's take her home," Pippa said. She set her doll in the car seat next to the baby. "Here, Penny, you can have her." Pippa's heart was swelling with a new, fierce kind of love.

Kim put the car in gear and pulled out of the parking lot. As she turned onto the road, Kimo started singing, "Your lyin' heart will put my song on the charts...."

And Pippa couldn't help but add, "And make me leave my baby in a car."

By the time they arrived at the house, Penny had begun to scream, and that was when they realized they had made a terrible mistake. They had left town and driven all the way home (through the forest to Wabo Point) without having bought any baby formula. Now it was late and the store was closed and the baby wouldn't stop screaming.

Toby exclaimed over her cries that they should give her baked beans, which were soft. Pippa bellowed, "Canned peaches!" Kim shook her head and threw open the fridge and pulled out the milk. While Toby rocked the baby, Kim warmed the milk, and Kimo and Pippa scoured the house for something small enough to use to feed her. In the end they carefully poured the milk into Penny's open mouth from a thimble.

But her screaming didn't stop! She was still hungry!

"One time I saw Lehua Madigan's mother feeding her baby a sausage," Kimo said.

"Lava gulls feed their babies fish," Pippa argued.

It was Toby who came up with the idea of mashing Cheerios into the milk because he liked to eat his cereal soggy and thought a baby might too. They tried this, and after a few bites the noise stopped. Sweet relief.

That first night none of them slept much. They were excited to have a new sister and they all wanted to hold her, plus it was finally spring vacation so they could sleep in if they wanted. Only they were wrong, they couldn't sleep in. The next morning,

Penny wanted them up! She was like one of those lava gull babies on the cliff face who cried nonstop out of hunger. She wanted to be fed all the time, and when she didn't want to be fed she wanted to be rocked, and when she didn't want to be rocked she wanted her diaper changed. Having watched the lava gulls for so many hours, Pippa was adamant that they should do whatever Penny demanded. "We don't want to be terrible parents," she said.

But the more they did what Penny wanted, the more Penny wanted them to do: more food, more rocking, more clean diapers. Kim couldn't believe how many things one little baby could add to her to-do list and how none of those things ever seemed to be completely done. She was ready for Penny to grow up already!

But Penny did not grow up. She stayed a baby all week, and it was a testament to the characters of the Fitzgerald-Trouts that they never once thought of returning Penny to her terrible parents. But that didn't mean they weren't going to argue about whose turn it was to take care of her. The feeding and the diaper changing were easy to divide up. Pippa offered to take Kim's to-do list and draw a chart that included those duties as well as Penny duty. After that, they took turns with all the tasks.

But holding Penny was a different matter. It was exhausting and endless, and it was hard to do anything else while they were holding her. It was hard to play drums or draw or swim or fish or read or make tropical drinks or do any of the things that the Fitzgerald-Trouts wanted to do. It was also hard to do the things they didn't want to do, like cleaning and cooking and driving. But if they put Penny down she would scream. So they tried not to put her down. But they were always looking for an excuse to hand her to someone else. Pippa was the exception; she proved to be the most devoted of any of them. Despite her small size and her thin arms, that first week she carried Penny for more hours than the rest of them put together.

By Sunday morning, Pippa had devised a little

sling out of an old bedsheet and some sailing ropes. She strapped the sling over her shoulders and carried Penny across her chest. This was enough to put strongman Kimo to shame. He offered to try carrying the baby that way. Once the sling was adjusted over his shoulders and the baby was in it, he had to admit that carrying her took hardly any effort at all.

Another thing they figured out was that Penny liked lying in a basket in the meadow listening to Toby play drums on the overturned buckets. She lay there holding on to her toes and listening to Toby's noise, while Kim, Kimo, and Pippa all snuck away and were able to spend a solid hour doing whatever they wanted (Kim reading, Kimo fishing, Pippa sketching lava gulls).

This quiet interlude came crashing to an end when Pippa spotted a lava gull hovering a few feet over Penny's basket. Its shadow wavered back and forth. It was making the lazy movement the lava gulls always made when they were about to swoop down on a fish. Little did Penny know she was about to be lunch. But Pippa knew.

She jumped to her feet in a rage and raced to the basket, throwing herself over her little sister. Toby saw what was happening and leapt up, brandishing his drumsticks. He waved them at the lava gull, who flew off in a huff.

By the time Kim and Kimo, who had heard the racket, came running, Toby and Pippa were holding Penny and looking triumphant. Over a lunch of toast, smoked oysters, and tapioca, Pippa and Toby told—and retold—the story of how they'd rescued Penny, and for a few hours after that the brothers and sisters were all nice to one another. But by that evening the mood had soured again.

They were sitting around a campfire on the edge of the cliff. Kim was cooking dinner and Kimo was holding the baby. Toby and Pippa  weren't helping with anything at all. Instead Pippa

was doodling and Toby was staring out at the stars and the full moon.

"Can't you guys do something useful?" asked Kim.

"You sound like a grown-up," said Pippa, who was truly exhausted by all the carrying she'd already done that day.

"This is useful," said Toby.

"Useful would be making toast," said Kim.

Toby kept staring at the stars. Something about them made him think about their conversation with Mr. Knuckles. Things had been so frantic since they'd discovered Penny that they'd never really had time to talk about what Mr. Knuckles had told them. Now Toby said, "What if the airplane doesn't have wings because it's a spaceship?"

Pippa gasped and Kimo yelped, but Kim shrugged and said, "No way."

"Yes way," said Toby.

"If that pile of metal is a crashed spaceship, then it has been sitting in the meadow for a thousand years. Does it look a thousand years old?"

"If it's alien metal," said Kimo, "it might not rust or get broken or worn down."

"The panels are round," said Pippa, "and spaceships are round."

Was it possible that aliens had crashed in their meadow? Stuck on Earth, unable to go home to their planet, they had started life anew on that island. They began families. They built homes. They developed a language and a culture all their own. In the process they named the place where it had all started, calling it Wabo for the shape of the dog's head they had seen as their spaceship crashed toward Earth.

If it were true, then the Fitzgerald-Trout children had discovered the greatest archaeological treasure of all time. An alien spaceship was proof not just of the origins of the island's first settlers, but proof of human contact with outer space!

"What should we do?" asked Kimo.

"It's an important discovery," said Pippa.

"We'll be famous," said Toby.

"We should report back to Mr. Knuckles's club," said Kimo.

"No," said Kim, "definitely not. Even if it were

true, which it's not, we *can't* tell anyone because if we told them, we'd have to admit we're living here."

They didn't all agree with Kim, but before they could launch into an argument, the smell of baby poo wafted over the campfire.

"It's your turn, Kim," said Pippa, consulting her chart by firelight.

"I'm cooking," said Kim.

"Here," said Kimo, pulling Penny out of the sling and holding her out to Kim. "Go for it!"

"Can't one of you do it?" Kim pleaded. "You're just sitting there doing nothing."

"I've been holding her for hours," said Kimo.

"You hardly notice," Kim countered.

"Then you hold her," said Kimo.

"What about you, Pippa?" asked Kim. "Change the diaper, will you?"

"I'm exhausted! I was up with her all last night." It was true. Pippa had done more than her share.

"Do it anyway!"

"I'll do it," said Toby, "but if I do, you have to let me tell the club about the aliens!"

"You can't tell the club." Kim was tired and frustrated. "Do you want us kicked out of this house and sleeping in the car again?"

"We can't live in a car with a baby," added practical Kimo.

"Not for some stupid grown-ups' club," said Pippa.

"It's not stupid," said Toby.

The smell was getting worse. "Just forget it," snarled Kim. "I'll do it! Like I do everything else!" She snatched Penny from Kimo. "And while I'm in there, I'll make the toast too," she said. "But I hope the fish burns. It would serve you all right to eat burned fish!"

With that, she stomped off across the meadow, leaving the others to feel their own feelings. To each of them it seemed so unfair how many chores they had to do. Unfair that they had to live this way. It was hard, at that moment, for any of them to imagine how they had ever lived together in a car. They didn't get along at all. Did they even like one another?

Inside the house, Kim laid Penny down on the couch, wiped her bottom, rolled up her dirty diaper, and put on a clean one. She went to the kitchen sink to wash her hands. See, she thought as she lathered with soap, I don't need those terrible mothers to tell me to wash my hands, I can remember to wash them myself.

She dropped two slices of bread into the toaster and went back into the living room to pick up Penny, who was squalling again. "Shush," Kim cooed, rocking the baby in her arms. Just then, Kimo, Toby, and Pippa came barging through the door, carrying the cooked fish.

"Something's burning," shouted Pippa.

"The toast!" Kim yelped and, holding Penny to her shoulder, ran to the kitchen counter to grab it. But the toast hadn't popped up. It was stuck; a thin curl of smoke rose from the toaster and swirled in the air above it.

Kim grabbed the toaster's lever and tried to force it up, but it was jammed. She tried again; no luck. She threw open the kitchen drawer, felt around in it for something, and pulled out a fork.

A *fork*? Anyone raised by decent parents knows to never, ever reach into a plugged-in toaster with a fork. But Kim had two terrible mothers and two (or maybe three) terrible fathers, and she knew nothing about toasters and forks.

*ZZZZZZAAAAAPPPPPPPPP!*

Electricity shot through the fork and into Kim's body, knocking her off her feet. Penny flew out of her arms and across the room. The baby was snatched out of the air by Pippa just as Kim hit the floor with a thud.

There Kim lay, her hair shocked straight up from her scalp, her arm blackened by the burst of electricity. Had her heart stopped?

The other Fitzgerald-Trout children crowded

around her, shaking her gently. Terror coursed through them. "Kim! Kim? Are you okay?"

Kim didn't move. She lay there like a stone.

Tears sprang to Kimo's eyes. His twin! How could this have happened? He pulled Kim up off the floor and held her to his heart, trying to rock her awake.

Still holding on to Penny, Pippa hugged Kim too.

And Toby grabbed Kim's hand, holding it tight, interlocking his fingers with hers. For some reason he whispered, "Plucky knucky make me lucky. Plucky knucky make me lucky." It was all he could think of by way of a prayer to bring his sister back.

They sat there like that: holding her, rocking her, whispering to her.

They could not imagine losing Kim. The oldest Fitzgerald-Trout. The leader of their flock. No matter how much they fought, no matter that they weren't all even related, they were brothers and sisters. They were Fitzgerald-Trouts, and they loved one another. They sat there, huddled together, tears leaking out of their eyes. For the first time all week, the baby's blistering cries did not seem out of place.

Then suddenly, as if she had been shocked again, Kim's eyes blinked open.

"She's alive!" said Kimo.

"Yes!" Pippa and Toby said at the same moment. Yes!

Penny stopped crying, and cooed and gurgled a little. She smiled a sweet baby's smile.

It made Kimo and Pippa and Toby smile too. They turned toward Kim and asked, "Are you okay?"

Kim's mouth tightened into a grimace. She sat bolt upright. "What happened?"

"You almost died."

"That's ridiculous," said Kim. "I wouldn't die. I wouldn't leave any of you, not for anything!" And she grabbed Penny from Pippa and she hugged that baby close. Then all the Fitzgerald-Trouts piled on top of one another, hugging and poking and tickling and rolling around on the floor until Kimo's elbow knocked Pippa in the nose and she jumped up, shouting, "Ouch!"

Kimo apologized and sweetly poked her shoulder to show he was sorry. "It's okay," Pippa said. They all knew that if you rolled on the floor and hugged each other, a little bruising was to be expected.

But what happened next was not to be expected at all.

There was nothing to prepare the children for it. There wasn't the sound of tires rolling up to the house, not even a knock on the door. There was no sound cue, just the front door suddenly swinging open. And into the midst of the ball of children on the living room floor stepped the one person they'd wished away, someone they wanted never to meet, the person they were sure would ruin everything.

That person, it just so happens, was me.

Let me back up a little bit and say that my
journey to the cabin on Wabo Point was not
as unexpected as it sounds. I had been visiting that
little cabin—kayaking there from my own house—
once a month for six years. I would open the door
with my key and look around the place. It was my
habit to make sure the electricity was still running
and the toilet was still flushing. I also checked
that the flag was flying above the roof. That was
my most important job! I'd been given a pile of

brand-new flags so that I could make sure there was always a bright flag flying over the house. It was something the owner had asked me to do when he left me the keys to the cabin.

"So you're not the owner?" Kimo asked, nervously taking a bite of his dinner. Once they'd gotten over their surprise at seeing a grown-up woman in their living room, the Fitzgerald-Trouts had offered me some fish. They felt so guilty at being discovered in the house that they thought it was the least they could do. I myself was so surprised to find them there that I waited until we were all sitting down to begin the conversation.

"Who is the owner?" asked Kim fiercely.

"I think I'm the one who should be asking questions here," I said. I could see that she wasn't used to talking to grown-ups. There was nothing pleasing or polite about her, but Pippa was worse. "Are you going to kick us out?" was Pippa's first question. "Are you?" Pippa was a little like a bloodsucking iguana. She might leap out at any time and sink her teeth into your flesh and not let go. "We have a baby, you know?"

"We have a goldfish too," said Toby, gesturing to the jug on the mantel.

"It's not my house," I said. "I'm taking care of it. I come here to check on things and sometimes to write."

"You're a writer?" asked Kim. She couldn't help but be interested. "Did you write that thing in the typewriter on the desk?"

"Did you read it?" I asked, suddenly angry at the intrusion on my privacy.

"She's a trespasser is what she is," said Pippa.

"She's right," said Kim. "We could report you. Send you to jail."

"I could report *you*," I said.

"No one would send us to jail," said Kimo.

He had a point. "I'm not a trespasser," I retorted. "The owner gave me the key. We're friends, the owner and I. It's you five who have some explaining to do. Just exactly who are you?"

"We're Fitzgerald-Trouts," they said in unison, and their eyes sparked like they were ready for a battle.

"Fitzgerald-Trout." I turned the name over in my mouth. "Any relation to Johnny Trout?"

"He's our father," they all said at once, then Kim blurted out, "Well, Kimo's father, but we're brothers and sisters anyway."

"If you have a pen and a piece of paper I could draw you a diagram, or we could go outside and I could draw in the dirt with a stick," said Pippa.

"We might be descended from aliens," said Toby.

I looked around at the group of them. Soulful Toby, with his black hair and his bright green eyes like a jungle you could get lost in. Fierce Pippa—the brown freckles on her face magnified by her enormous glasses. Kimo, the bighearted strongman with a baby strapped to his chest. And Kim, as stern and competent as any headmistress. I was already imagining how I would describe them. I was already inspired. I could see myself crumpling up the paper in the typewriter and starting something new. "I've read about kids like you," I said.

"You must have read *The Awfuls*," said Kim. She was wiping the last of the fish off her plate with a piece of toast. "We're a lot like them."

"I hate that book," I told her. But I didn't tell her why. The reason was personal and I wasn't about to explain it.

"*The Perfects* is worse," said Pippa. "The most boring book ever."

"You've got that right," I said, thinking I might turn out to like Pippa best of all.

"Anyway," said Kim, "I guess we'll be going." She stood up and began collecting the dirty dishes. "Please don't tell the owner we were here. We'll leave everything very tidy. It won't take us long to pack the car." The others rose to their feet and together they started sorrowfully toward the kitchen.

"Wait," I said. "Where are you going?"

"To clean the house and pack up the car. If we leave right away we'll get to our parking spot on the beach before bedtime." This was Kimo.

"Don't leave yet," I said. They all turned to look at me, their heads tilted in confusion. (I swear, even the little baby had her head tilted; she was becoming one of them.)

"You're Johnny Trout's children, right?"

"That's what we just said."

"Well, you should know that this is Johnny Trout's cabin."

"His cabin?"

"He doesn't have a cabin. He's lost at sea!"

"He does have a cabin," I said. "He left me to look after it. You don't recognize it at all?"

"For as long as any of us can remember," said Kim, "we've lived in the little green car."

But a look of wonder and clarity was washing over Kimo's face. "The siren," he said. "That's where I've seen her. It wasn't on a boat. It was here when I was little. Maybe I lived here?" Kimo was understanding for the first time in his life that he had, at one time, known his father.

"I think I remember you," I said. "Johnny had a baby when he was with that tacky singer. Is she your mother?"

"Yup," said Kimo, and then nodding toward Toby and the baby, "theirs too."

"So you're the one Wendell hated." I was talking to Kimo.

"Wendell?" he said.

Then I told him about Johnny Trout's pet pig, Wendell. Johnny had been given Wendell when Wendell was a tiny little piglet and Johnny had raised Wendell by feeding him scraps off his plate. Johnny loved to sail and whenever he went sailing he took Wendell with him. They would anchor overnight and Johnny and that pig would both sleep on the boat. They got very close. Eventually, the pig started sleeping in the house.

"So that little door in the back, it's not a dog door?" asked Kim. "It's a pig door?"

"I thought it was for a tig—" started Pippa.

"What do you mean Wendell didn't like me?" Kimo interrupted.

"Wendell tried to attack you in your crib. They couldn't set you down anywhere without Wendell trying to take a bite out of you. That pig was jealous. That's why when Johnny split with your mother he didn't want to keep you."

"He chose a pig over me?" Kimo's heart was sinking.

"What did you expect?" Pippa shook her head defiantly. "He's a terrible parent, just like the rest of them. It would've been better to have been raised by lava gulls."

"I'd still like to meet him," Kimo said. "I'd like to tell him what I think of that." Kimo sounded fierce, and he was holding the baby very tightly like he wanted nothing more than to protect her from just such a father. In fact, that was what he was doing.

"So you're watching Johnny's place while he's at sea." Kim turned to me.

"I live on a little island two miles off the coast," I explained. "I come over when it's a full moon and the tides are favorable. When Johnny left on his sailing expedition six years ago, he asked me to take care of the cabin and to keep the flag flying over it. He and Wendell are steering a course toward Wabo Point. He wants to see the flag when he gets within sight of the island."

"You make it sound like he's still alive," Pippa said.

"Alive, dead, I don't know," I said. "But I promised to keep the flag flying. Maybe he's just taking his time."

Kim had moved across the room and was standing just above me. She looked down with a face so serious it could have been carved from stone and set as a monument in our town square. "So while you wait for Johnny to return, can we live here?"

"He wouldn't like it," I said. "He didn't even want a baby living here and now there's a baby and four more."

"But he's not here," said Kim.

"Neither is Wendell," added Kimo bitterly.

They were right about that. And for reasons of my own, I wanted those children to stay in that house a little while longer. I saw a chance to finally write something I could be proud of.

"I guess a man who is lost at sea can't object," I said. "But if he comes back, you're going to have to skedaddle."

"What's that mean?" asked Toby.

"You'll have to move out," I said.

"For now, we can stay," said Kim, a hint of victory in her voice. And then they were all talking at once, loud as a flock of lava gulls, saying things that I wouldn't come to understand for a while, about drums and swims and baths and blenders and beds, and how now they wouldn't need to buy new tires for a long time.

Kimo took the baby out of the sling and they passed her around, kissing her on the forehead and saying it had all happened because of the good luck she had brought. Kim lifted Goldie's jug off the mantel and kissed its glass, saying the goldfish had had a part in it too. Then I had to ask, "What did the fish do?"

"He's part of the reason we found the house," said Kim, and she began to tell me their story.

CHAPTER
17

When Johnny Trout left on his sailing canoe trip he told me I could use the cabin as a place to write, but I never managed to produce more than that one bit of writing that Kim found in the old typewriter. It was the beginning of a story based on my relationship with my twin sister, Stella. She was born only two minutes before me, but somehow she got all the luck. She became a successful children's author, best known for her two-books-in-one bestseller, *The Perfects* and *The*

*Awfuls*. I had also set out to become a writer. But I never managed to write a whole book. Instead I'd taken a job writing jokes for the TV show *Ham!* because it brought in the bacon (an old *Ham!* punch line).

But writing sausage jokes is the würst (another *Ham!* punch line).

You can imagine what a pleasant surprise it was to discover that after an evening of listening to the Fitzgerald-Trouts, I wanted to write their story.

I began to visit the children at the cabin on Wabo Point. I went once a month when the moon was full and the current between my island and Wabo was not too strong. When I got to Wabo,

I would pull my kayak up onto the beach, climb the path up the cliff (holding on to the spice bushes), and then—before settling down with the other children—I'd take Penny for a quick walk through the meadow. I figured the others would be more likely to tell me the details of their story if I did something helpful. They could be very prickly and very private children. When I felt they were really resisting giving me information, I did something even more calculating. I made them ginker cake.

Ginker is a rare spice made from the roots of the ginker plant that grows on Mount Muldoon. The root has to be dug up when the ginker is flowering, and the ginker flowers only once in its life for an hour or two. Sometimes I had to hike for miles before finding a ginker root I could use. But baking ginker cake turned out to be an excellent ploy to get the children to tell any parts of the story they were holding back. This was how I got Kim to admit the details of her mad scheme, details she had never told her brothers or sisters.

Lest you think I was so terrible, I did do a few things to help them out, such as making sure they were trained in the proper use of all the cabin's appliances and helping them type out the application for Penny to go to Windward Childcare Center. Toward the end of each visit, I would take out my notebook and I would get them to tell me the story of the jail or the goldfish or the night at MARRA. And so, like a snake swallowing its own tail, this story should end with all of us in the living room eating ginker cake while I take notes on the story of my own arrival.

But it doesn't end there, because something happened that meant the story wasn't even close to being over.

They were in the laundromat, arguing in low voices while they watched Penny's dirty diapers go around and around in the washing machine.

Toby, who had become quite vocal over the last few weeks, was making a plea to his siblings to tell Mr. Knuckles and his club about the spaceship in the meadow.

"It's not a spaceship," said Kim.

"How do you know?" snarled Toby.

"We won't ever find out unless we tell him." Kimo took Toby's side.

"Why are we talking about this again?" groaned Pippa, who was bouncing Penny in her arms. "I'm sick of it. I thought we agreed we couldn't tell him because of the house."

"That doesn't matter anymore. I don't care who finds out we're living at Wabo Point," said Kimo. "We're allowed to be there unless Johnny Trout and that nasty pig come back."

"But it's nuts," said Kim, getting up and banging on the broken vending machine with one hand and reaching inside it with the other. She pulled out a candy bar and began to unwrap it. "It's nuts to think we're descended from aliens. Nuts."

"No it's not," said Toby. "Look at those people in the picture. They all think so."

"They're dumb grown-ups," said Kim. "Have you looked at that picture? Do you know who's in the IDIOTS club?"

"It's IDOOS," Toby corrected her, looking very offended.

"Whatever it's called," said Kim, feeling bad that she'd once again been mean to Toby, "have you seen who's in it?" They all shook their heads. "Tina's terrible husband. The man in the blue convertible with the matching blue tuxedo."

"The man who might or might not be our fifth parent?" asked Pippa.

"Yes," said Kim. "He's one of them."

"You're kidding!" said Kimo.

"You'll know him by his bright red scalp!" Kim nodded toward the photo on the wall. "Go and look."

So they did. One by one they got up and stealthily walked past Mr. Knuckles, who had the newspaper spread out on the counter and was engrossed in the word Jumble. They didn't want him to know what they were doing. One by one they came back and sat down and nodded at Kim. She was right. The man in the blue convertible was there, all right. They passed around the chocolate bar.

"It's a bad idea anyway," said Kim. "No offense to Mr. Knuckles, but we're not aliens. We're humans. I feel human. Look at me, I'm human!" And with that, Kim ripped off a piece of chocolate and shoved it into her mouth and scratched under her arms like a gorilla, shouting, "Human! Human! Human!"

Toby snatched the chocolate bar from her. "I feel like an alien," he said.

"Me too," said Kimo.

"Me too," said Pippa, looking surreptitiously at Mr. Knuckles, who was scratching his tattoos, still stuck on the same word in the Jumble. "Unless we tell him about the plane or the ship or whatever that metal thing is, we will never know."

Kimo nodded in agreement and said, "I vote yes."

"Yes," Pippa said, but Kim was shaking her head.

"You!" Pippa suddenly lost her temper. "Don't get to decide *everything*!" Pippa pressed the baby to her chest and covered her ears, then let out a piercing scream that terrified Kim.

Mr. Knuckles looked up from his Jumble and wrinkled his brow.

"All right," Kim said quietly. "Have it your way."

And so it was that the Fitzgerald-Trout children found themselves a few days later in their car, waiting for the members of IDOOS on the road near the turnoff to the Sakahatchi Forest.

The children had confessed their discovery to Mr. Knuckles and he had been impressed and intrigued. He had sent emails to all the members of the group asking them to meet in this spot and promising an exciting afternoon. He had not told them exactly what they would be seeing. He did not want the newspapers catching wind of the discovery until the club had confirmed that the metal parts belonged to an alien spaceship.

It was midafternoon and the children were there early (as children often are) and were annoyed to be waiting for a bunch of tardy adults. Kim sat behind the wheel, reading one of the nautical novels from Johnny Trout's collection while the others passed around a thermos of tropical punch. "I'm not even sure why we're doing this," Kim said, looking up from her book.

"Don't fight it," said Pippa, passing the thermos to Toby.

"Penny needs her nap," said Kim.

"Don't make excuses," said Toby. They weren't used to sitting in the car for long stretches of time anymore and they got grumpy very quickly.

"We could wait outside," said Pippa. "We don't have to sit in the car. We could stretch our legs."

"Too late," said Kimo, who had caught a glimpse in the rearview mirror of a convoy of cars heading down the road. "Looks like they're here."

The children all turned around and watched as the cars drew closer.

"Oh, gross," said Pippa, adjusting her glasses. "Look who's leading the charge." The blue convertible with its open-air top was at the front of the line of cars heading toward them. The driver was actually wearing the blue tuxedo as if he expected a ceremony instead of a scientific trek. "Abandoning a baby. I can hardly look at him." Pippa shook her head with disgust.

As the cars pulled up into the clearing beside the road, the children could see that all the members of IDOOS were wearing suits and fancy dresses. Perhaps Mr. Knuckles had told them to be ready for a photo op.

The grown-ups were clambering out of their cars, and so the Fitzgerald-Trouts climbed out of theirs. Kim was swinging open the door when she spotted Tina. Quickly Kim got back into the car and took off her stew-can shoes. She was very proud, and she could not bear the thought that Tina, in her fabulous cowboy boots, might see Kim wearing those stew-can contraptions. As soon as her shoes were off, Kim slid out of the car and joined the group of adults.

Mr. Knuckles had his camera out and was trying to get a photograph of the group, but the man in the blue tuxedo, who had his arm around Tina, was wagging a finger at him. "As president of this club, I demand that you tell us why we're here!"

"I tell you when we get through forest," said Mr. Knuckles. You could tell he didn't like the president.

"That's not good enough," said the tuxedoed man.

"You tell him, Clive!" shouted Tina, her bouffant quivering above her head. The children all looked at one another. At last they knew the man's name—it was Clive! Pippa was thinking how this would be useful to know when Penny was older and asked who exactly her father was.

Clive was clutching Tina and she was nibbling his ear, and all the time the two of them were indifferent not only to Tina's two older children (Kimo and Toby) but to her newborn baby as well.

"All right, all right," Mr. Knuckles was saying. "Fine, fine. I tell why we here."

"You bet you will," said Clive, grinning a

greasy grin. Kim thought he looked greasy all over, right up to his oily red scalp, like he hadn't had a bath in years.

Mr. Knuckles had begun to speak. He was telling the club members about the children's discovery of the wrecked aircraft with no wings. Toby looked like he was going to burst with excitement. If Kim had been closer to him, she would have poked him and reminded him to breathe.

When Mr. Knuckles had finished describing the wreckage, the members of IDOOS rushed to their cars. Here was the proof they had waited for for so long! They could not get there fast enough.

"Stop!" shouted Clive, and everyone froze. They turned to look at him. "As president of this club, I have a right to inspect this wreckage before anyone else."

"You tell 'em, Clive!" Tina shouted, and took another little bite at his ear.

"Our car will go first," he said. "The rest of you can follow." Mr. Knuckles and the others grumbled, but there wasn't much they could say. Someone had to go first and it might as well be the president.

"You"—Clive turned to look at the children—"can lead me in your car." Up until that moment Kim wasn't sure Clive and Tina had known they were there, and now she was speechless at the thought that they had known and hadn't cared to even say hello.

A woman in a sequined dress blurted out, "What about the iguanas?" Everyone looked at the children, but Clive harrumphed, "Old wives' tale!"

"I don't know," said the woman. "I've heard details."

"Me too," said another.

"Yeah," shouted a third.

"Roll windows up," advised Mr. Knuckles.

"Good!" agreed the others, but Clive's car had no roof, no windows. He turned to the children and said, "You've been riding through the forest, haven't you?" All the members of IDOOS were listening.

"Yes," said Kim.

"Every day," said Kimo.

"A lot," said Toby.

"Any iguanas ever bite you?" asked Clive.

The children all hesitated. What should they say? Then Tina burst in, "Clive, honey, I'm too terribly busy for this." She turned on her heel.

"Come on, if they'd been bitten we would know. There would be scars."

"You're right, babe." He smiled his greasy smile and walked with her toward the convertible. The children just stood there. Tina was so terrible and so dismissive, they couldn't bring themselves to contradict her.

Kim climbed into the little car first. She pulled her door shut and was about to put on her stew-can shoes when she felt something against her feet. She looked down. "Hey, look at that," she said to Kimo. "I can touch the pedals."

It was true. At last her legs were long enough to drive.

She turned the key and threw the car in gear. The other children were all turned around in their seats watching what was happening behind them, but Kim, who was a very careful driver, didn't turn around. She looked in the rearview mirror, and that was how she saw the blue convertible pull out onto the road behind her.

Ryan Lizzo had been right. The iguanas were so fast Clive and Tina didn't even see them coming. *Snap! Snap! Snap!* Those thick, bloodsucking green missiles rained down on the open-topped car and snapped their teeth deep into the flesh of Tina and Clive. *Snap! Snap! Snap!*

"She's got an iguana on her arm!"

"He's got one on his nose!"

"One's biting his ear!"

"I think that's Tina." Pippa began to laugh her frightening laugh.

Clive had stopped the car and now more and more iguanas rained down on the convertible. The air was thick and roiling with them. The convertible seemed to be filling up. The children could see that Clive was trying to turn around, but so many iguanas clung to his flesh he couldn't get a grip on the steering wheel. Somehow he got to his feet and leapt out of the car. Tina leapt out too. They began to run away from the forest and toward the IDOOS cars with their windows rolled up. Someone in one of the cars had a phone out and was calling an ambulance.

That was the last thing Kim and the other children saw as they drove off into the woods.

CHAPTER
18

On a cloudy day many weeks later, the children were up on Mount Muldoon digging ginker root to make a cake for a school party. They were scouring the hillside for the plant's fragrant flowers. As they walked, they talked about that great afternoon in the Sakahatchi Forest. It wasn't the first time they'd talked about it. They had discussed it over and over until it had become the stuff of Fitzgerald-Trout legend.

They talked about how Tina and Clive had

been taken to the hospital—scarred, but alive—and about the song Tina had recorded from her hospital bed ("Iguana Gonna Getcha"). They talked about how they couldn't believe the song was number two on the charts. Toby compared it to another kind of number two, which made the others laugh even though they knew it was immature. They talked about how after that, Tina and Clive had both been spotted wearing brand-new pairs of iguana-skin boots.

Then they talked about how later that same afternoon, the other members of the IDOOS club had converged in the meadow and stood, dumbfounded and silent, staring down at the wrecked aircraft that might or might not be a spaceship. They had taken photographs. They had drawn diagrams. They had labeled and numbered all the metal parts. And then they had carefully packed the ship into cardboard boxes and loaded the boxes onto a truck and sent them off to a lab to be studied.

When the trucks were gone, the club members

had told the children it would be years before they could confirm whether or not the wreck was an alien ship.

Standing there on Mount Muldoon, sniffing the air for ginker blossoms, the children groaned and spit on the ground. "Why did they have to make things so complicated?" complained Pippa. "Tests, research, more tests, they're never going to find anything out."

"Whatever they find," said Kimo, "it won't matter. They'll argue about it. They'll have conferences in the fancy hotel. They'll publish articles."

"They'll make careers out of saying aliens or not aliens," said Pippa.

"We never should have shown it to them," said Toby. "Idiots is right."

"Grown-ups ruin everything," said Kim, and Penny, who was slung across Kimo's chest, giggled.

"Hey, look," said Pippa. "A ginker flower." She had spotted a blossom growing on a ledge a long way down the mountainside. Lurching off the path toward it, she lost her footing and stumbled, knocking Toby from his feet. They both landed with a thud in the soft grass and then, before they could think, gravity had taken over and they were rolling down the hillside, gathering speed as they went.

Standing on the trail, Kim could hear their laughter careening off the mountainside. Before she knew what she was doing, she dropped to the ground, lay flat on her side, and launched herself down the hill too. She rolled and rolled and rolled, laughing harder and harder. Somewhere on her wild ride down the hill, the little notebook that had once held her to-do lists fell out of her pocket, never to be found again.

When they reached the base of the hill, Pippa, Toby, and Kim lay there laughing and catching their breath. Kim felt her heart banging pleasantly in her chest. "I am, I am, I am," it said, and everything in Kim answered, "Yes!"

Kimo, with Penny in the sling, appeared, standing above the others in the grass.

"You've got to see this," he said.

And that was how all the children found themselves perched on the mountain's edge looking out over the island. It spread before them like a map. They could see the foot of Mount Muldoon, where they had parked, and they could see farther away to the laundromat and their pavilioned school. "Look," said Kimo, and he pointed out across the island beyond the coastal road and the Sakahatchi Forest. "Do you see what I see?" It was the peninsula of Wabo Point, sticking out into the ocean. Wabo Point with its distinctive coastline. "You can see Wabo from Mount Muldoon," Kimo explained. "That's how they knew it was shaped like a dog."

"I told you we didn't come from space," said Kim.

"We just feel like it," said Pippa.

"Because we're Fitzgerald-Trouts," Kim agreed proudly.

The five Fitzgerald-Trouts looked at one another and grinned. Then Kimo bent down to dig at the root of the ginker plant, and Toby and Pippa got out knives to help. Only Kim stood looking out over the island and to the ocean beyond.

And that was why Kim saw what the others did not see. A tiny white spot on the horizon that she thought might be the sail of a canoe headed for Wabo Point. She couldn't tell yet whether the sail had the picture of a dog's head printed on it or not. Was trouble heading for them? It was impossible to tell. But from what Kim knew of life, there was always some sort of difficulty ahead. They had made it through a lot already, and they would face whatever came their way.

Kim looked away from the tiny boat and back at her brothers and sisters. The ginker cake would be delicious. She would start baking it as soon as they got home.

# THANK-YOUS

Thanks first and foremost to the oldest four Fitzgerald-Trouts—Kim, Kimo, Pippa, and Toby—who shared their stories with me. And an extra thank-you to Pippa, who picked out the book's font, Stempel Garamond. Many thanks to the readers (young and otherwise) who made this book better: Caroline Adderson, Douglas Fudge, Jozy Liftin-Harris, Finnegan Sanders, Graley Sanders, Kristin Sanders, and Linda Spalding. Thanks to my fellow writers at *Ham!*—Semi Chellas, Tassie Cameron, Gillian Deacon, and Hilary Liftin—whose notes were invaluable. Thanks to the wonderful Sydney Smith, who drew the island and its inhabitants just exactly as they are. Thanks to my agent, the amazing Jackie Kaiser, and to my editor, the incomparable Susan Rich, who has spent a good deal of time on our island and helped me get the details right. And to my daughter, Gemma Fudge, without whom this book simply would not exist.

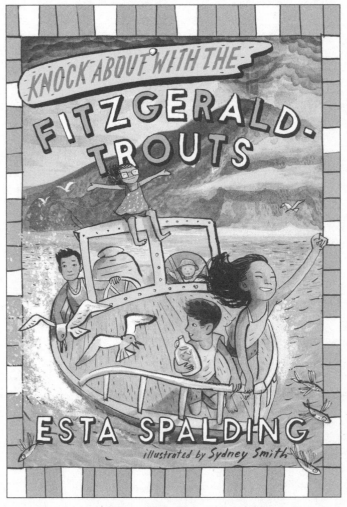

CHAPTER
1

Kim Fitzgerald-Trout might have been only eleven years old, but she was a very experienced driver, so as she turned onto the road that descended the dark slopes of Mount Muldoon, she slowed her little green car. Her four brothers and sisters were laughing into the darkness around her, repeating lines from the movie they'd just seen at the drive-in. It was only the first week of summer vacation but they had already been to the drive-in twice, which meant that Kim had driven the same road only a few nights before. Still, she drove carefully. The road was surrounded on all sides by a forest of maha trees. Kim didn't want to risk an accident in the battered old car whose engine made a gurgling noise even when it wasn't driving down the steepest mountain on the island.

Kim's brother Kimo, who was the second oldest and sat beside her in the front of the car, saw her fingers clenched on the steering wheel. He nudged her gently with his shoulder, his way of asking if everything was all right. "It's too dark," Kim answered, flicking on the high beams that illuminated more of the road.

"Well done," Kimo said in a phony English accent, and they all laughed appreciatively. It was a line from the movie they had just seen called *The Nosy Ninja*, about a basset-hound ninja who solved crimes by sniffing out the villains. At the end of the movie, the nosy ninja had discovered the stolen diamonds stuffed into a rump roast being overcooked in an oven. That's when the police inspector had patted him on the head and said, "Well done, nosy ninja. Just like this rump roast."

Pippa, who was eight years old and sat in the backseat behind Kimo, shook her fist in the air and repeated the villain's last line from the movie: "You oughta mind your own business, nosy ninja."

"The nose knows," Toby, the second youngest, said, making a sniffing noise just like the basset hound, then pretending first to smell the jar that held his goldfish and then the bald head of Penny, his baby sister, who sat beside him in her car seat. Penny cooed gleefully, letting loose a slurry of spit-up onto her doll, Lani.

Most children, when they leave a drive-in movie theater, go home and get in their beds and go to sleep, but the Fitzgerald-Trouts were not most children. When they left the drive-in, they stayed in their car, which was their home and which gave them the freedom to go anywhere they wanted.

At night they parked at a campsite beside Pea

Tree Beach where they slept under the stars and swam in the morning, cooking their oatmeal breakfast over a familiar campfire. They all had gotten used to this setup and had even begun to enjoy it. But not Kim; she was adamant that they should live someplace more permanent. Kim was very fond of to-do lists, and the number one thing on her to-do list was *Find a house*. She had done this once before, when she'd led her siblings through dangerous woods and found an abandoned cabin on Wabo Point. The owner of the cabin had turned out to be Kimo's father, Johnny Trout.

Now Kim glanced over at Kimo and saw that he was looking at her too. They were only a few months apart in age and their names were almost the same, so they liked to think they were almost twins and could read each other's minds. Maybe they could, because at that moment Kimo was also thinking about the cabin on Wabo Point and how things had gone so wrong when his father returned. A look of worry clouded Kimo's face.

"Don't," Kim said quickly, then changed the subject. "Why would anyone hide diamonds in a rump roast?"

"I'd hide them in a freezer with some ice cubes," said Kimo, grateful to be thinking about something besides his father. "Or maybe I'd hide them in a bank."

"Smart," said Toby.

Pippa wiped her glasses on her T-shirt and scoffed, "You wouldn't steal them in the first place. You're not a villain."

"But if I were..." said Kimo.

"You wouldn't be," said Pippa, putting back on the glasses that magnified the dark freckles around her eyes. "You're not greedy. Villains are always greedy."

"Villains weren't always villains," said Kimo. "Something happened to them to make them that way."

"Spoken like someone who will never be one," snorted Pippa, just as a bright flash of light pierced the windshield. Kim threw a hand up over her eyes. She could hardly see the road now, but between her fingers the light flashed again. She blinked as if blinking could make the flashing stop, but it couldn't, and for a second she was driving blind. She hit the brakes, steering toward the shoulder, where the little green car rumbled to a stop just as Toby yelled from the backseat, "Look at that!"

Toby was pointing to a creature standing some distance away in the middle of the road. The creature was human in its dimensions but made entirely of metal that glinted in the moonlight.

Kimo shook his head and said, "Are we dreaming?"

"Probably an alien," said Toby, who had always hoped to meet one.

"Alien schmalien," scoffed Pippa. "I don't think an alien would be carrying that." She pointed to the long object that dangled from the creature's hand. It was an ax. Kim, who was a great reader of books, thought the creature looked like the Tin

Woodman from Oz, though it seemed to her to be made of a softer kind of metal.

"Whatever it is, it's heading toward us," said Kimo, suddenly nervous. "Roll up your windows! Hurry!" He saw that the metal man was waving its free hand in the air. "What do you think it wants?"

Before any of them could answer, the creature called out, "Help!"

Kim tightened her grip on the steering wheel. What to do? She looked at Kimo and asked, "Should I drive?"

"Please, help!" the creature called out again, and Kimo thought how it would be irresponsible of him to let a giant metal man carrying an ax get any nearer to his brother and sisters. On the other hand, he and his siblings had had their own share of trouble in life and were sympathetic to anyone (or anything) that called out for help. "Let's keep the windows up and ask what it wants," Kimo said to Kim.

Kim nodded, and rolled her window down a

crack, shouting to the creature, "We want to help you, but put down your ax or we'll drive away!" The creature, now only a few yards from the car, did as it was told, setting the ax down on the muddy shoulder of the road and raising its hands in surrender.

"All right," said Kim, "you may approach." She was speaking very formally, as if this might defuse the bizarre situation. The metal man took a few more steps toward the car, but just as it was about to reach them, a loud shriek rose up from the maha trees that bordered the road. The children turned and saw the dark sky full of even darker wings. Thousands of birds—screaming and cawing—had suddenly flown out of their nests and were circling above.

"What's going on?" This was Toby, who nervously clutched the jar that held his goldfish, Goldie.

"Something scared them," Kim reasoned.

The metal creature was outside the windows

now, banging on the glass. "Let me in before it starts!"

"What starts?" Kim shouted back.

"Knockabout!" the metal man shouted just as there came an earth-shattering rumble, the sound of millions of tons of rock being torn apart, the sound of the planet's vast and ancient tectonic plates shifting. The metal man was right; it was a "knockabout," which was what the inhabitants of the island called an earthquake.

The car began to buck like a horse. Its tires were jumping up and down. Then, suddenly, everything around the car was moving, even the road. The maha trees swayed so that first one branch then another bent and touched the ground. It was as if a giant had picked up the earth and was amusing himself with it. Turning it this way and that way. Shaking it. Playing with it like a toy.

Strapped in her car seat, baby Penny began to wail with fear. Pippa, who felt a ferocious and protective love for the baby, scrambled out of her own seat and slid down in front of Penny's so that she could face the baby and hold her hands, comforting her.

Meanwhile the metal creature was outside the bucking car, trying to hold on. It gripped the door handle and shouted, "Let me in!"

Forgetting himself, Kimo reached into the back and flipped up the door lock. The back door swung open, and instantly the metal creature moved into the churning vehicle.

For several long seconds the car bucked up and down, bouncing the children and the metal man around inside it. Then, just as suddenly as it had started, the shaking stopped. Everything went still: the car, the road, the trees. Even the birds stopped their shrieking and quickly disappeared back into their nests in the maha branches.

It took a second for the children to catch their breath and realize the knockabout was over. The danger had passed. It took another second for them to realize that the metal creature was now in the car with them. So the danger hadn't passed. During this second, the creature reached its metal paws up and, with a little tug, began to pull off its metal head.

Toby screamed and covered his eyes, so he didn't see what the others saw: The creature's "head" was really only a big, soft metal mask—like an inside-out oven mitt with eyeholes cut from it. Underneath the mask was the face of a grown-up. She had long black hair and bright green eyes. She was smiling. "You can always tell when something big is coming. The birds fly out of their nests all at once like that. They sense it."

"Sense what?" asked Kimo, who was no longer afraid.

"A knockabout," said Kim, catching the woman's meaning.

"There have been more and more of them lately."

"Yup," the children agreed, almost in unison. They had noticed it too. There were knockabouts every few days when the whole island seemed about to capsize, like a fragile boat tossed on the ocean's surface.

"Thanks for stopping," said the woman, whose enormous eyes made Kimo think of satellite dishes. "My name is Leaf."

"Are you a space alien?" asked Toby, who had uncovered his eyes and was sounding hopeful.

"I'm a scientist," Leaf said, looking around at the patchwork of children. They had varying degrees of brown hair and brown skin. Some had black eyes and some had green.

"Scientist?" Pippa was confused. "What's with the getup? You look like something from a horror movie."

"I study plants that grow around the crater of the volcano," Leaf answered. "This is a lava suit. I wear it so I can get close to the volcano and take samples of the plants without getting burned."

"There are plants that grow on volcanoes?" Kimo had studied volcanoes in school and didn't remember hearing about that.

"Of course there are," said Leaf, opening her eyes even wider. "You should know about volcanoes. You're an islander."

"He's a Fitzgerald-Trout," said Kim. She didn't like the way the woman never seemed to blink, but just stared at them with those flying-saucer eyes.

"Whoever you are. You should know about the place where you live. You should know that volcanoes destroy most plants completely." Now Leaf's voice dropped to a whisper so the children had to lean close to hear her. "If you don't know that, then you won't be able to help when you're needed."

"*Needed?* Who needs us?" This was Toby, whispering into the air. Kim and Kimo looked at each other, unsettled.

But Leaf didn't answer the question. Instead she said, "Mount Muldoon has started leaking lava. It's a dormant volcano, but it's woken up. Ask the birds—they fly out of their trees whenever the lava comes."

Kim noticed that Leaf's eyes sparkled as she

said this; the woman seemed to be excited at the thought of the volcano spewing fiery liquid rock. The thought made Kim shudder. "We'd better get out of here," she said, starting the car.

"Wait," said Leaf, opening the door. "Let me grab my ax." The children looked at one another. They didn't trust grown-ups, especially grown-ups with axes. Pippa, who had a temper that rivaled even the fiercest volcano, growled at Leaf, "You have to put your ax in the trunk." Her

brown freckles darkened as she spoke, making her look like she might explode.

"All right," said Leaf, giving a small shrug and running to get the ax.

"Well done," Kimo said to Pippa, then added, "just like this rump roast."